I0689370

THE *Clause* REBELLION

Also Available From Elizabeth Lee Sorrell

Wrong Turn Fairy Tales

Gwynn worked hard to live up to her family's expectations putting away all childish things and even a few childhood friends. Now she is about to marry Addison, a very sensible, very rich businessman, but before she can say yes to his proposal, she finds herself falling through one fairy tale after another. Will she find her happily ever after with her very  own prince charming, or has her fairy tale taken a wrong turn?

Exclusively found from Barnes & Nobles for Nook Book.

More Than Instinct

Kat had a past best left forgotten. Jackson had a past he couldn't get over, but when circumstances throw them together in a dangerous game, they had to find a way to work together. What they would find was that, "This whole mess had bonded them in a way that could never be undone." 

Available from your favorite bookstore.

THE *Clause* REBELLION

Elizabeth Lee Sorrell

trading as

Yarbrough House Publishing

Acknowledgements

I'd like to thank my family who really do all the hard work. While I sit back and make up fanciful stories, my family stays busy proofing, formatting, illustrating, crunching numbers, and taking care of all the "business stuff." All I do is play with my imagination, but my family works hard to bring life to my stories.

Chapter One

Wynter sighed with frustration. She had been trying to tell her dad about her day, but he obviously didn't have time. Nothing unusual there. She couldn't remember the last time she had actually been able to talk with her dad.

Why have kids in the first place if you don't have time for them? That could be why her parents had decided to only have one child.

Wynter stepped outside and sighed again. At least if they'd ever had more kids, Wynter would have someone to talk to out here in this barren waste land. There was nothing here but snow and ice. There were no wild animals of any kind unless you traveled to the water. That would mean having to cross the human settlements, though; no human had ever been able to find Santa's workshop in the North Pole. The only sign of life in this part of the North Pole was Wynter, her parents, and the elves.

Sure, there were a lot of the elves, but they were always busy making toys. They had to keep up with demand, and each year there were more and more kids who were demanding more and more toys.

Her mother said it took a lot to run a large scale operation like the one they had going in the North Pole. She was far too busy to spend quality time with Wynter. Oh, she tried. She would spend time talking with Wynter as she cooked meals or cleaned.

Magic was really Wynter's only source of entertainment on a daily basis. Wynter reached her hand out as it started to snow and caught the snowflakes in her hand with a mischievous smile.

"Wynter!" Santa bellowed from his office.

Wynter skipped up the stairs with a victorious smile. She had his attention now.

"Yes, Daddy?"

He glanced up briefly wearing an aggravated mask. He may not have been very happy, but at least he had noticed her.

"Fix that," he said pointing in the direction of his fireplace.

Wynter smirked at the fireplace. It was snowing inside the fireplace, and the flames had been extinguished. With a wave of her hand, the snow stopped and the wood and ashes dried up. Then a flick of her index finger started the flames once more.

"All better! Guess what happened today!"

"Not now, Wynter. You know what's at stake if we fall off schedule. Go tell your mother."

"But…" Wynter huffed and left the office slamming the door behind her. She had just started a roaring fire without matches in the middle of this frozen tundra, but she supposed it was asking too much for Santa to notice.

"Wynter Lynn, stop slamming doors. Don't make me come up there," her mom hollered from downstairs.

Yeesh, Wynter needed a life. She was twenty-one and resorting to childish pranks to get her father's attention, and her mother still talked to her like she was ten. It was time to get out of here. Where would she go though? Her father kept an eye on what was going on all around the world. He would find her in no time, if he took the time. The only place he didn't watch was… the South Pole.

The South Pole! It was brilliant. The North Pole and South Pole had never gotten along. No one would ever think to look for her there. Plus she wouldn't have to hide her magic. The South Pole families had magic as well, just not as strong. She wouldn't even have to adjust to the climate change; cold was cold.

Satisfied with her decision, Wynter started packing. It wasn't hard to hide. She didn't even bother shutting her bedroom door. No one cared what she did as long as she stayed out of the way. She left a note on her bed if anyone bothered to look for her, because let's face it, leaving and letting her parents believe something horrible had happened to her was just plain immature. She didn't tell them where she was going, in the note, but she did tell them that she was fine and not to worry.

Maybe running away wasn't very mature either, but Wynter desperately needed to find her own way in life. As soon as she was packed, Wynter scurried out into the cold with her bags. She slipped behind the toy shop where no one would see, and she used magic to transport to the South Pole.

The South Pole looked much like the North Pole. Ice, snow, and more ice, but here there were signs of life everywhere. Wynter could see tracks where a rabbit had crossed the snow covered ground. There was a polar bear trying to catch diner. The humans didn't believe that there were bears, or much life at all for that matter, so deep south, but what did the humans know? They didn't believe there were magical beings either, but here she was. You would never convince the humans that there was an entire magical community living at the South Pole, so why would she bother taking the time to convince them there were animals they didn't know living at the South Pole?

Wynter loved that the animals lived in such close proximity to the South Pole people. It was fascinating to watch them, and there were no animals, sans the reindeer, to watch at the North Pole. She watched the bear with curiosity for some time.

He slunk over to a hole in the ice, crawling on his belly. He was covered in white fur with only his little black nose poking out. His matching black eyes were intent on watching the hole where he must have spotted a seal. It was the cutest thing that Wynter had ever seen. Then the bear waited. When the seal it was tracking was forced to come up for air, the bear snatched it right out of the water using its powerful jaw. Once he had the seal, the bear started tearing into it like he was starved. It was a gruesome way to die and a gory meal, yet Wynter still found the polar bear enduring and adorable.

Finally after watching the polar enjoy his meal, Wynter moved to explore. She found a cave right away that would be perfect for her to stay until she could find something a little more permanent. She wasn't sure how long she really wanted to stay here. Mostly she just needed some time to herself, time to think. She had a lot of things to sort out if she was ever going to figure out her place in life.

A little magic made the cave quite comfy. Temperature control for one was a must, and comfortable furniture wouldn't hurt either. A little work and the cave resembled a home. Her parents wouldn't have thought much of it. The truth was they would never dream of setting anyone up in something so primitive, yet it was enough for Wynter. It was her own home, and she was proud of it.

Over the next few days Wynter ventured out exploring the land. Finding food was tough. She had never had to hunt for her own food before. Her dad probably could have used magic to get food, but that was well past Wynter's ability. She wasn't as strong as her father magically, and she never would be. Clause women were never as strong as the men. That was why the job of Santa was always passed down from one male to another.

Wynter had no idea what her parents planned to do about the fact they had no male heir. They never talked about it, at least not in front of her, and they never gave her the chance to ask about it. Maybe her dad believed that he could go on forever. Who knew?

Of course her mom was only a Clause by marriage. She wasn't all that strong at all, at least not magically. Wynter could run circles around her mom in a manner of speaking. Wynter wasn't exactly stunted in her magical ability; she just wasn't as strong as her father. There was no shame in that. At least she knew that her parents wouldn't be trying to pass the family business down to her.

That was something she certainly didn't want. Who in their right mind would want the job of Santa? Year round stress, stringent deadlines, demands of a material driven world, the strain of making it all around the world in one night. Nope, it was not Wynter's cup of tea. Speaking of which, a nice hot, cup of tea would be just the thing to warm her. Oh if only.

With a wiggle of her fingers a bow appeared in Wynter's hand. She had never been much of a hunter. Who was she kidding? She had never hunted a day in her life. She pulled the string back; more like she tried to pull the string back. It took more muscle than she had expected. It took her several tries to get the string pulled back, and it took her hours of practice before she hit anywhere near a target.

A very large target the size of an iceberg. She would never be able to hit prey. At this rate she would starve to death. Wynter sat down on the ice covered ground to sulk. She just had to survive on her own somehow.

She sat there for a long time watching a seal periodically poke his head above the water through a hole in the ice. He would come to the surface, take a breath, look around, and dive back under the water. He was actually pretty reliable with his timing. If Wynter had been any better with the bow, she might would have stood a chance of catching diner.

Slowly a polar bear loped up, looking about curiously. He spotted Wynter but did not react right away. He watched her, and Wynter was careful not to do anything to startle the bear. Soon the seal caught the bear's attention. They both watched the seal. The bear must have noticed the same thing Wynter had about the seal's timing, because he started to slowly belly crawl across the ice. He paused just before the seal came up for air. Staying low and still, the bear avoided drawing the attention of the seal.

The seal dove back underwater, and the bear picked his belly crawl back up. This time the bear crawled right up to the hole and waited for the seal to reappear. After that it was an easy capture. The seal was enormous, impressively large as far as seals go. It would make a more than adequate meal for the bear; in fact, Wynter would wager that the bear had more than he could eat in one sitting. It wasn't like the seal would keep until the polar bear's next meal. Anything left over would just go to waste. As far as Wynter knew, however, bears were not naturally inclined to share a meal.

With a gentle wave in the bear's direction and a bit of magic, Wynter had the bear's undivided attention.

"Mr. Bear? That's an awfully big seal you've caught there. You did a fine job hunting."

The bear looked down at the seal lying dead at his paws and back up to Wynter.

"My name is Wynter. I've always wanted a pet, but my parents thought it unfeasible. Would you mind if I called you Roscoe?"

The bear moved his head from side to side in an obvious attempt to answer.

"Do you like the name?"

The bear wagged his head up and down in the affirmative.

"Great, then your name will be Roscoe. I'm very hungry, and you have more meat there than you can eat. Perhaps you would share a little with me?"

The bear made no move to answer, but instead he started dragging the seal over to where Wynter sat, leaving a bloody trail in its wake. It was a gruesome scene. The hole in the ice was surrounded by blood where the seal had been killed then a trail of blood spread from the scene of the crime, to edge closer to Wynter.

Wynter shook her head. She mustn't think like that. She eagerly built a nice fire with a flick of her wrist with a grilling rack to stand over the flames.

Wynter had not thought about a knife to cut the carcass with. Obviously she was going to have to fashion herself a stove as well as cooking and eating utensils. Before she could conger up a knife, though, Roscoe tore off a hunk of meat and tossed it to her fire.

"Oh, thank you!"

Wynter placed the meat on the grill then used snow to wash the blood from her hands. She watched the bear tear into what was left of the seal. "I could cook that for you if you'd like," she offered.

A huff from Roscoe was answer enough that Wynter didn't offer again.

Roscoe had finished off the seal and already begun to wash his paws and muzzle in the snow by the time Wynter had finished cooking her portion of the seal. Roscoe sat down next to Wynter; it was now his turn to watch her eat.

When Wynter was finished eating and all cleaned up, Roscoe laid down right up against Wynter's hip. She leaned back into his side, and together they enjoyed a peaceful sunset.

"You know," Wynter whispered into the quiet of the night, "I've always heard that polar bears were particularly vicious, but you are rather friendly. I'd still like to offer you something in return for sharing your meal with me...Could I offer you a warm place to sleep?"

Roscoe stood up and nudged Wynter to her feet. Walking back to her cave, Roscoe stayed right on her heels just like a loyal dog, a very large breed of dog.

When they got to the cave, Roscoe looked around and vigorously shook the snow from his coat.

"Oh, Roscoe! You're getting snow everywhere. Next time do that before coming inside." Wynter blew air out between her lips as she turned a circle looking around the now wet cave. Instantly all the wet snow dried up. "There all better."

Roscoe curled up on the floor at the foot of Wynter's bed. Unable to resist, Wynter wrapped her arms tightly around Roscoe's neck and cooed, "Good night, Roscoe."

Chapter Two

The next day Wynter set out early with Roscoe. He caught a walrus for breakfast, and this time Wynter was much better prepared. She cut a chunk away from the carcass and threw it over a roaring fire.

Roscoe didn't eat as much of the walrus as he had the seal the day before. He must have still been full of seal. Wynter knew that the walrus meat wouldn't keep long, so she cooked what was left.

Holding a piece of the perfectly grilled walrus out to Roscoe, Wynter cooed, "Don't you want to try just an itty bitty bite?"

Roscoe sniffed all around the meat before easing his way up to the walrus meat in Wynter's hands. He sniffed the meat and huffed.

"That's fine. You don't have to eat it. I can eat it later," Wynter taunted.

Roscoe sniffed the meat again then quickly gobbled it up.

"See? That didn't kill you, did it? Was it good?"

Roscoe nudged Wynter with his nose. Next he gave her a playful shove to the ground and walked over her to get to the remainder of the meat. In less than two minutes there was nothing left of the walrus meat.

"Wow," Wynter laughed. "I thought you weren't very hungry."

Roscoe loped a few feet from Wynter and looked back expectantly.

"What are you up to?"

He moved a few more feet and looked back for a second time. This time Wynter stood and followed. Roscoe made a gruff but nonthreatening sort of growl and began moving again. Wynter followed at a quick pace. She didn't know where they were going but Roscoe seemed to know.

They walked for a pretty good way before Roscoe stopped. Wynter moved to stand next to Roscoe and gasped when she took in the sight before them. In front was a large open area where a sleuth of six polar bears played.

"Oh, I don't know if this is such a good idea. I should head back to my cave."

Wynter turned to leave, but Roscoe shoved her hard enough to knock her to the ground. She landed on her butt with a thud. The hard ice made the fall feel rougher. Before she could get back to her feet, Roscoe growled loudly, very loudly.

The head of every bear snapped to attention, all eyes on Roscoe and...Wynter. Wynter watched the bears unsure if she could put the same spell of understanding on all six bears at once that she had put on Roscoe.

One by one the bears slowly started walking toward Roscoe and Wynter. Wynter who was still sitting on the ice was terrified. What was it they told you to do when you find yourself face to face with a vicious bear? Play dead? It was a little too late for that.

Roscoe let out another small growl and nudged Wynter. Was he offering her to his friends? Was he showing her off? What was he doing? How was she expected to understand the mindset of a bear? Her understanding spell only allowed him to understand her speech, not the other way around.

The bears continued their slow advance until they were close enough to touch. They circled around Wynter, and she knew this was where she was going to die. Death by bear mauling. Why oh why did she ever mess with a polar bear?

The bear directly in front of Wynter sniffed at the collar of her coat and bared a fang. Roscoe roared and swiped at the offending bear. He didn't swing hard enough or with enough claw to do damage, but it was enough to make a point. He was...warning the other bears?

The bear that Roscoe took a swing at loped away, but the other five remained curiously checking Wynter out. Wynter carefully watched Roscoe as he carefully watched the other bears. One of the bears touched Wynter's cheek with his cold nose, and she flinched. Roscoe reacted to Wynter's flinch with a low warning growl.

Eventually all the bears went back to their play, leaving Wynter alone with Roscoe. He nuzzled her neck with his snout, and then he ran off to play with the other bears. Wynter let out the breath that she had been scared to let go before. She practically folded in on herself and cried. She cried until she had nothing left in her.

He had been warning them. They knew what she looked like now. They knew her scent. She still wouldn't be in a hurry to ever see them again, but all the other bears knew now that she was with Roscoe. He had staked his claim on her.

Roscoe played chase and tackled the other bears. They tackled him. All the while they communicated with grunts, growls, and roars, even a few snorts. Wynter waited until her weak from fright muscles could hold her up again then pushed to her feet. Still afraid to turn her back on the heard of bears, Wynter eased backwards.

Roscoe whined when he caught Wynter's movement out of the corner of his eye.

"It's ok. I'm going back to the cave. You go ahead and play with your friends. I'll see you later."

Roscoe whined again. He looked at the other bears, back at Wynter, and started walking toward Wynter.

"It's ok, really. You don't have to walk me back. I'll be fine," but still Roscoe strolled away from his friends. "You big goof, I told you I'd be alright," Wynter insisted as she hugged Roscoe. Roscoe didn't resist when she hugged him, and Wynter knew that she had found a best friend in the most unlikely of beasts.

Most days Roscoe and Wynter traveled out to see his friends. The other bears gave Wynter a wide birth, but Roscoe was accepted easily. Wynter was happy to see Roscoe play. He was light hearted and care free, yet Wynter felt just as lonely and left out here as she had at home. She sat alone most of the cold lonely days. She was eager for evening to break when she and Roscoe would go back home to the cave.

Roscoe lived with Wynter in the cave now where he had his own bed to lay on at the foot of Wynter's bed. She had been here for two weeks now. She enjoyed her new found freedom, and she loved spending time with Roscoe. Each day that she knew him she only loved him more. He was her gentle giant. He loved to wrestle with her and play rough, but it was a different kind of play than what he played with the other bears. It was like he was more careful with her for which Wynter was eternally grateful.

No matter how much Wynter enjoyed her freedom and being with Roscoe something just wasn't right. She was still lonely in a way. She missed human contact. Even though she was ignored at home, at least there were other humans there. Of course there were humans here too. The only problem was that at the South Pole people would just as soon kill her as look at her.

Once again something had to give. Wynter needed more. Each day she began slowly venturing out further than she had the day before. She remained quiet and snuck around so as not to be caught by any of the South Pole inhabitants. Creeping from snow drift to snow drift on light feet, Roscoe soon decided that their daily excursions were a game.

He would sniff around until he caught the scent of something that piqued his interest. Then he would follow the trail until the scent faded out. After following one such trail one morning, Wynter began to hear voices. She crouched down behind a snow drift with Roscoe by her side and peeked around the snow to see where the voices were coming from.

In a small clearing, stood two boys. It was hard to tell their exact age or even an approximate since the North Pole and South Pole people did not age the same. The Clause family tended to age much slower than others, but if she had to guess, Wynter would think that the boy was in his late teens while the younger one was still a preteen.

"You're not showing me right," the younger boy moaned.

"I'm showing you exactly how to do it. You're not following my example," the older one replied. He was tall with dark hair sticking out of his cap. Something about the way he moved captured Wynter's attention and would not let go.

"Dad said you're supposed to teach me," the younger boy pouted. It was adorable the way his bottom lip jutted out just enough to appear pitiful. His young, round face was full of frustration and disappointment. Whatever it was that the other boy was supposed to be teaching, the younger one wanted badly to learn it.

"I'm trying to teach you, but you won't listen."

"I am listening."

"Well if you are listening, you're not doing it just the way I said."

"I did what you said the best I can. Everything you say doesn't make sense, only some of it."

"See? That's why I say you're not ready yet. If you can't even understand it yet, how are you going to do it?"

"I could understand it if I had a better teacher," the younger boy challenged.

"Yeah? Go find yourself a better teacher. Then I won't have to waste my time trying to explain it to you."

"No, Dad said you have to teach me."

"Fine, in that case, try it again."

"I can't try it again. I don't know what to do."

"It is simple. The snowball is already balled up for you, and it's not like I'm asking you to throw it or anything. Just levitate it a foot off the ground. It's like you're picking the snowball up nice and slowly. A foot is all you have to do this first time. Stop whining, Noah, and just try it."

"I am trying it!"

"That's pathetic."

"It's not pathetic, Ethan! Dad says I'm doing good."

"Doing good? You're not doing anything."

"At least I'm trying."

"Yeah, yeah. We'll try again tomorrow," Ethan said as he levitated the snowball and lobed it at Noah's head.

Wow. So these were real live South Pole inhabitants. Brothers by the sound of it. Noah was adorable, but Ethan was…striking. He was very attractive.

Ethan said that they would try again tomorrow. Obviously Ethan was supposed to be teaching Noah how to use his magic. Theirs must not work the same way as the Clause family magic, because if it does, then Ethan is teaching it all wrong. He wanted Noah to think it through, but for Wynter is was a feeling. She had to know what she wanted to do then just feel it bubbling and let it happen.

Oh well, either way, Wynter wanted to come back tomorrow to watch them again. "Come on Roscoe. Let's go…Do you think you could find this place again tomorrow morning?"

Roscoe bobbed his big head up and down, and Wynter smiled contently, excited that she would get to see the boys again.

Wynter was so excited that she hardly slept that night. She kept tossing and turning wondering what the boys might do the next day.

The next morning, Wynter hurried through breakfast and rushed back to the place where she had seen the boys. Roscoe found the opening with ease, but the boys were nowhere to be found.

"They said that they would practice again today. We'll just sit down for a few minutes behind this snow drift and wait."

Roscoe curled up, and Wynter snuggled into his side. She was nearly asleep when the distant sound voices made it to her ears. Forcing her eyes open, she pushed up and peeked over Roscoe's back. Roscoe snorted and went back to sleep. He had not been very happy about being kept up all night. One thing that Wynter had noticed about bears was that they did tend to sleep a lot.

As Roscoe slept, Wynter lay across his soft, cushy body and settled in to watch the boys.

Ethan swirled his hand in the air, and snow flew off of the ground, into a ball, and gently back to the ground. "Okay, close your eyes," he told Noah. "Now, I want you to picture the snowball on the ground. Can you see it?"

"Yes."

"Can you imagine what it would feel like in your hands?"

"Cold," Noah answered blandly.

"What else?"

"Wet?" Noah wasn't sure of himself.

"Okay, that's good. What else?"

"Round. I don't know. What does this have to do with anything?"

"Just shut up and do what I tell you," Ethan barked at his younger brother.

"Fine, but this is stupid."

"What else?"

"A waste of time."

"Not that, stupid. What else can you imagine about how the snowball would feel in your hands?"

"Round is all, I guess."

"Okay, cold, wet, and round. I want you to imagine it lifting off the ground now."

The snowball did lift off the ground then. It wasn't far, only a couple of inches. It was not impressive by Clause standards, but since the young child couldn't lift it at all the day before this was at least an improvement.

"Open your eyes," Ethan smiled.

Noah opened his eyes slowly. When his eyes took in the floating snowball, his mouth dropped open and his eyes grew wider. "I did it!" he exclaimed.

As soon as Noah made the explication, the snowball fell abruptly back to the ground. It didn't discourage Noah, however, who was too busy jumping around and screaming at the top of his lungs.

"Okay, okay. You levitated it a couple of inches. That's a start, but we still have a long way to go. Try it again." Ethan was trying to sound firm and unaffected, but even he was delighted over his brother's triumph. He was trying desperately to hide a smile, yet he couldn't keep the sides of his mouth from curling upward ever so slightly.

He had an interesting smirk, and Wynter was sure that his full on smiles would be just as fascinating or more so. Wynter watched as his smirk faded and was replaced with a frown. A glance at the snowball told why.

The snowball was sitting completely stationary where it had smacked back onto the ice. Noah's face was contorted in effort, yet the snowball did not budge.

"Stop, stop, stop," Ethan exasperated, and Noah's face fell weighed down with disappointment. "You're over thinking it. When you lifted it just now, was it hard?"

Noah thought for a minute. "No, I don't think so. I didn't even know I was doing it."

"Exactly, relax, and just let it happen."

It was a wonder Noah got it off the ground at all. Ethan was confusing. One day he's telling his brother that magic is mental instead of physical, and the next day he's telling his brother not to over think it. If it was all mental, didn't Noah need to think it through? For Wynter magic was hard to explain. If she had to lump it into a single category, it would probably fit best into emotional. That wasn't to say that there wasn't a mental and physical aspect to it as well; it was more emotional though.

Noah took a deep breath and let it out in a whoosh. His shoulders slumped, and he gave himself a loose shake. He stared at the ball. Wynter did not know what was going on inside that kid's head, but there was nothing outwardly showing.

Ethan waited patiently as Noah stared at the ball. Ethan was much more patient today. Noah was much more focused today. Wynter did not know how long they stood there motionless. Noah stared at the snowball, and Ethan stared at the ball. Wynter took the opportunity to study Ethan.

She had a closer vantage point today and could get a clearer look at his face. He had full lips that wore a slight pout when he concentrated. His large grey eyes were framed by dark, impossibly long lashes. How was it the case that guys always got the long lashes while girls had to apply globs of mascara to get the same look?

His eyebrows were thick but well defined. Wynter doubted that Ethan had spent any time purposely defining them. Wynter trimmed her brows up, magically of course, at least once a week. She couldn't stand the idea that they might take over her face. Not that her eyebrows had ever been particularly unruly. It all stemmed from something she saw on a cartoon once when she was little, and she had worried about it ever since.

His complexion was darker than what Wynter would have expected from someone from such a cold climate. It was darker than her own by quite a bit. Her own skin was most comparable to porcelain. His face was free from any blemishes, freckles, or any other distinguishing marks. Wynter had a sprinkling of freckles across her nose and cheeks; it was a part of her Clause heritage as was her amber hair. Amber wasn't really red hair. It was far from a beautiful auburn color. It was a weird smashing of red-orange and brown, but that was not a worry for long. If she took after her father's side of the family, as she so often did, her hair would turn white at a very early age.

Noah was a cute kid. He had high cheek bones and chubby cheeks. They were the kind of cheeks that some people wanted to pinch. Personally those chubby cheeks made Wynter want to kiss them. Maybe it was because her father had chubby cheeks like that. She always loved kissing her father's chubby cheeks, because he always paid attention when she kissed his cheek.

He had dark hair like Ethan, but his eyes were bluer. They were a very pretty blue, not at all like Wynter's plain brown eyes. Her eyes were the color of coffee. Her mother always said they were the color of melted chocolate, but all Wynter ever saw when she looked in the mirror was coffee.

Noah's eyes almost disappeared when he smiled. Wynter never had that problem since her eyes were so large; doe like is what her mom called them. Noah had an innocent smile. Wynter bet it was hard to stay mad at Noah with that innocent looking smile. His smile must have been natural too, because even deep in concentration there was still a smile on his face.

Ethan watched Noah without letting any emotion slip onto his face. His grey eyes were mesmerizing. Wynter could feel herself getting drawn in, but she just couldn't muster up enough will power to care. She almost leaped out of her skin when Ethan suddenly started laughing.

Noah pouted, and it took Wynter a moment to notice the smashed snowball laying crushed on the ground.

"Don't worry about it, kid," Ethan continued to laugh. "It took me a while to get it right too. You've made good progress today."

"But, it's pummeled," Noah pointed out in a defeated tone.

"True, but at least you made some kind of change. That's better than yesterday, right?"

"I guess."

Ethan used magic to form another snowball then launch it directly at Noah's head.

"Hey!" Noah reacted with a smile as he hurriedly reached down to gather up a snowball of his own. Both boys took cover when a full scale snowball fight ensued.

Wynter watched the boys having fun, and she desperately wanted to join in. The only playmates she had ever had growing up were the elves. They hardly had any more free time than either of her parents, and it just wasn't the same playing with the elves.

Wynter knew better, however, than to approach the South Pole people. They may look friendly enough, but that would all change if they saw a Clause. Wynter had never understood what the reason for the feud was between the North Pole and South Pole, but whatever it was it was serious. If Wynter were to approach the carefree South Pole boys, their playful game would turn violent in seconds, and all that violence would be aimed at Wynter.

So, Wynter settled for merely watching the game and living vicariously through the boys.

Quickly Wynter ducked down as a stray snowball began sailing in her direction. Unfortunately the snowball hit Roscoe, who woke up with a roar. The last thing you want to do is startle a bear. Roscoe stood up on his hind legs staring at Ethan and Noah, roaring and growling.

Noah screamed, and Ethan's face froze in a mask of fear. "Noah, get out of here. Go get help," Ethan ordered. He kept his body perfectly still positioned between Roscoe and Noah.

Noah took off at a run, and Ethan started slowly backing away never taking his eyes off Roscoe. Roscoe took a threatening step toward Ethan. He was still growling deep in the back of his throat.

"Shh, it's ok. It was just an accident. Calm down...If you let the boys go, you and I can go back home and I'll cook you a nice big seal. You would like that, wouldn't you?" Wynter cooed into Roscoe's back.

Roscoe let his growl trail off, but he continued to watch Ethan. Wynter knew, though, that Roscoe was going to let him go. Roscoe had become very fond of cooked meat, and seal was his very favorite.

Ethan continued backing away at a snail's pace until he was out of sight. As soon as he was out of sight, Wynter heard his feet pounding on the ice as he switched into a fast sprint. Roscoe fell back to four legs and started a happy trot toward home to catch a seal. Roscoe may have detested being startled awake, but this time, at least, the payout had been worth the price.

The boys didn't venture that far out after that day, and Wynter couldn't blame them. If their positions had been reversed, she would have done the same thing. She no doubt would have stayed far, far away from where she had become a potential meal for some enraged polar bear. They had no way of knowing that Roscoe wasn't all that dangerous. He had become more of a house pet than a wild bear. The only vicious moments he ever had any more was when he was hunting food.

Chapter Three

It happened one morning that Roscoe woke Wynter early. This was strange, because Wynter was usually the early riser. She was always the first one up since Roscoe was such a deep, sound sleeper. He would sleep late into the morning.

Roscoe nudged Wynter's face with his cold, wet nose, and he pawed at her side until she rolled over and hummed, "Hmm?"

He pawed at her once more with a little more force. "Okay, I'm getting up. What is it?"

It was odd for Roscoe to get up so early, yet it was odder still that he would be so insistent that she get up. If he needed to go out, he could get out easily on his own. The cave was only shut away from the outside world by a magical wall. She and Roscoe could walk in and out as easily as if it was not there at all, but it still kept the elements at bay. It even had concealment. They could see out, but you could not see in from outside. From the inside it looked like a large all glass door, but from the outside it looked like just any other empty cave.

Roscoe went to the mouth of the cave and looked out intently. Wynter forced her eye lids to open wider. Then she saw it. Outside the cave everything was white. Well, it was more so than normal. The ground was always white, but this morning even the air was white. Outside a blizzard was raging.

Wynter knew that blizzards could be dangerous, but they were so beautiful. Roscoe was content to sit there and watch, so Wynter sat down next to him and burrowed close sharing his body heat.

The wind was outrageous. At first the snowflakes were small, like a fine powder. The wind was blowing so hard that all you could see was the fine powder snow blowing about. It was like you could visibly see the wind blowing across the frozen plain. It swirled this way and that in a whirlwind of chaos.

For a brief time the wind started making a circle that made the snow appear to be hitting the ground then flying straight back up. It was a curious thing. Wynter could see the appeal of waking a friend to sit and watch the storm with you. The blizzard had an almost magical quality.

After they had been watching for more than an hour the snowflakes started getting larger. The large flakes were traveling parallel to the ground as the wind blew them in a fast, straight line. Soon they were accumulating swiftly on the ground at the mouth of the cave. The snow was growing taller right before their very eyes until finally there was nothing but a wall of snow in front of the cave shutting them inside.

Wynter stood and stretched out her stiff muscles. Thankfully she had added a fridge to the cave and, she and Roscoe had worked dutifully to fill it with food in case of just such an emergency. "How about some breakfast?" Wynter asked.

Roscoe's bear-sized appetite nearly emptied the fridge, but that was just fine. That's what it was there for. Wynter knew from experience that some frosty mornings were simply too cold to get out in. On mornings like this, it was nice to have food in the fridge and not have to go catch breakfast in a snowstorm. Of course they would have to refill the fridge later that day, but Wynter was eager to get out and see the effects of the storm anyway.

After breakfast was cleaned up and Wynter was bundled up nice and warm, she and Roscoe made their way out of the cave. Wynter had to use magic to create a strong hollowed out tunnel as they went. The tunnel took them right up to the surface. It was still snowing with small scattered flakes.

The first thing Wynter noticed upon exiting the tunnel was the wind. The wind was still stout. It pushed Wynter back immediately. She wasn't ready for the sheer force of the wind, and she would have been knocked down or possibly even blown away if it had not been for Roscoe planting himself behind her and stopping her backward momentum. She ducked her head and pushed forward. It wasn't a lot of fun fighting the wind, but it must have been a great workout.

It wasn't until the wind died down some time later that Wynter and Roscoe could really get a good look around. Roscoe dug his claws into the side of a mountain of a snowdrift and climbed his way to the top. He stood at the top of the snowdrift and stretched his neck upwards watching the flurries still falling all around him.

While Roscoe watched the snow fall, Wynter laid down in the snow to make a snow angel. It was childish and ridiculous for someone who had lived all her life in a frozen tundra, but she just couldn't resist the urge to play in the snow after a snowstorm. She was like a child on Christmas morning, which had never been all that great for her.

Wynter wouldn't see her dad for over a week before Christmas Eve, due to all the last minute preparations. He was that busy, that even though they lived under the same roof, she literally wouldn't lay eyes on him for over a week. In fact, it was very nearly two weeks. Most families spent Christmas day together, but not her family. Her dad would sleep all day. Her mom tended to the overworked elves, and Wynter was expected to tend to the reindeer.

Wynter had always spent a great amount of her life with the reindeer. Maybe that was why it felt so natural to have an actual polar bear as her best friend now.

Pushing all the sobering thoughts from her mind, Wynter set to work on a snowman. With hard work and a bit of a magical touch, she built a snow bear that bore a resemblance to Roscoe. It had been her intention to make a snow bear replica of Roscoe, but her artistic ability left much to be desired. It was a strong enough resemblance that it could have been a family member.

Roscoe sat down and slid down the snowdrift. He stood up and stopped in front of the snow bear. He studied it closely then with a snort walked away. Guess he didn't like it.

Roscoe bowed his head and pushed his nose into the snow. Then the silly bear plowed forward leaving a trench in his wake. The full grown male bear was playing just like a cub. Wynter loved his carefree personality. He was so fun loving, he brought joy into Wynter's life that she hadn't been sure she would find anywhere in the North or South Poles. Coming here had been a good decision simply for the good fortune of meeting Roscoe.

They played in the snow for hours like a couple of kids, or more like a kid and her dog. They were quite the pair. If only her dad could see her now. Surely the sight of Wynter playing in the snow with a huge polar bear that had basically been domesticated would make him laugh.

Wynter missed that jolly laugh. She had missed it for years now. It was missing from her life long before she ran away. That old poem that people used to recite was dead on; his belly did shake when he laughed exactly like a bowl full of jelly! It was the perfect description! Whoever the author was must have caught a peek at Santa.

He used to laugh all the time. Little slip ups at the workshop would make him laugh. Now days all they did were make him grumpy. Jokes at the dinner table used to make him laugh. Now days if he actually sat down to a family meal, jokes only made him testy. A funny face used to make him laugh too, but now they just make him cranky. He never has time for "such nonsense."

That was the thing about it. He never had time for anything anymore. The stress of the job was really starting to get to him, but he didn't have an heir to pass along the responsibility to, at least not a male heir. Who's ever heard of a female Santa Clause? No one, that's who, because there has never been a female Santa Clause.

What a disappointment Wynter must have been. An only child and not even a boy. Suddenly not in the mood to play anymore, Wynter started back for the tunnel that would take her to the cave.

Roscoe had not noticed yet that she had walked off, and she wasn't paying much attention to where she was walking. Before she knew what had hit her, she had walked right into something and bounced backward to the ground. Wynter looked up to see a very startled Ethan turning to see who or what had just bumped into his back.

"What are you doing out here? Don't you know there's a blizzard?" Ethan demanded.

Wynter's heart raced as she realized that she had been caught. There wouldn't be any going home after this. They wouldn't release a Clause; the hate ran too deep.

"I could ask you the same thing," Wynter deadpanned.

A small smirk crept across Ethan's face. "Do you live around here?"

"Yes," which was the truth. She did live around here now. He had not asked if she had always lived around here.

"Are you out here alone?"

"I have a pet with me somewhere." Wynter didn't mention what kind of pet.

"That's cool. We don't have a dog." Ethan must have assumed that her pet was a husky or some other cold adapted dog. She wasn't going to correct him. "My little brother was out here, but he chickened out when the wind knocked him down. Do you have any siblings?"

"No, I'm an only child."

"That must be nice, no little brothers to annoy you."

"No, actually it is rather lonely."

"You have your parents though? It must be awesome to not have to share their attention."

"I don't share their attention, because they are too busy to notice me."

"Oh. You want to hang out with me for a while? Unless you were busy..."

He wanted to hang out with her? Didn't he realize who she was? He must not! He thought she was from around here, from the South Pole. Of course there were no physical differences between the North and South Pole people. The only thing that could actually give her away short of a slip of the tongue was a display of more magic than any of them possessed. All she had to do was play it cool and keep her magic under wraps.

"No, I wasn't busy."

"Great. My little brother and I were going to start a snowball fight, but he's not all that good at magic yet."

"Oh...um-" Wynter couldn't possibly tell him she could do it. She had to keep magic out of this!

"I'm sorry. I didn't mean to- Don't you know how to use your magic?"

Wynter wasn't sure how to answer that. Was it unheard of for the South Pole people not to use magic by this age?

"I guess your parents didn't have much time to teach you, huh?" Ethan asked sympathetically.

Wynter gave a shrug. Her dad had taught her the basics when she was young, but as she got older she had been set out on her own and told, "Practice makes perfect." She had stretched her limits through trial and error to see just what she was capable of.

"I could teach you," Ethan offered eagerly. "I mean if you want to. You don't have to. I guess you want to get home, huh?"

He was offering to spend time with her, and he was eager to do it. There was no way Wynter was going to turn that down. "I'd like that if you're sure you don't mind."

"No way! It will be fun! So, how old are you anyway? Fifteen? Sixteen?"

Was that how old she looked? She had almost forgotten how differently they aged. "Sixteen," she lied.

"I'm nineteen. Name's Ethan."

"Hi, Ethan. I'm Wynter."

"Cool name."

"I guess." Wynter had never given her name much thought. It was what it was, but if Ethan liked it, she had at least that to thank her parents for.

"I'm teaching my little brother right now too. Don't worry. You won't have to practice with him or anything. So...I started him out trying to levitate a snowball." Ethan twirled his finger pointing at the snow, and a snowball formed on the snow fluffed ground. "It isn't as easy as it looks. When I was learning, I must have crushed a hundred or more before I finally got one to levitate."

Sneaky thing. He didn't tell his brother that little tidbit, but really, how hard was magic for the South Pole people? Wynter could do simple levitations as a toddler. She had to make it look difficult, though, if she didn't want to be caught.

"Ok, so close your eyes," Ethan instructed. "Picture the snowball in your mind's eye."

Wynter followed Ethan's directions just out of curiosity since she knew nothing would come of it.

"Can you see it?" Wynter nodded. "Good. Now picture it literally lifting off the ground and floating there a couple inches off the ground."

Wynter pictured the snowball levitating. Then out of sheer boredom she pictured that same snowball rolling back and forth along the ground and then exploding.

"That's funny."

Wynter opened her eyes to look at Ethan curious what was so funny. He was staring at the snowball like it had grown wings and flown away.

"Your magic should be strong enough by this age to at least cause the snowball to twitch, even if you have let it go unused for so long."

What was he talking about? Magic was not a use it or lose it sort of skill.

"Ok, let's try this." Ethan moved around behind her. His warm heat engulfed her immediately. Aligning his arms with hers, he lifted her arms out in front of her. "Close your eyes again. This time I want you to imagine reaching down and actually lifting the snowball."

He was wrapped around her, embracing her like a hug. All Wynter could think about were Ethan's strong arms beneath her own, and they were strong. The same as she was older than she looked, he was stronger than he looked.

"Are you imagining it?" he asked, breaking her out of her revelry about long, sinewy muscles.

Wynter nodded, and Ethan continued. "Good. Now let everything else go, and just let it happen."

Obviously he expected something to happen, but not too much. Wynter lifted the snowball off the ground the barest inch, and Ethan exploded with excitement.

"You did it! Open your eyes and look. It's levitating. You're a natural!"

A natural? He had no idea. Her mother had often complained that Wynter would magically throw random objects across the room as a mischievous two year old.

Levitating an object a mere inch was more like an infant exploring their world where she came from.

Ethan quickly spun Wynter around in his arms and hugged her close. "That was great!"

"Thank you," she replied trying to sound flattered. She wasn't flattered, more like flustered. Man, it felt nice when this guy held her tight. He barely knew her, yet he looked so proud. The look of pride that blanketed his face was humbling in a way despite the fact that what Wynter had just done was so pathetic. She liked knowing that she had made him proud.

"I...uh...I should probably get back home. I'll have to help with clean up after that blizzard," Ethan told her.

"Oh, ok."

"Do you want to meet again tomorrow?"

"Yes!" Did she sound too eager?

Ethan gave her a blinding smile. "Good. We can meet here. I'll be out here pretty early to train with my brother. I'll wait for you...so...whenever you get here."

"That would be wonderful."

"I'll see you tomorrow then."

Wynter watched him walk away. He looked back once and waved. It wasn't until Ethan was well out of sight that Roscoe loped up to her side and whined.

"What? I don't begrudge you time with your own kind, now do I? Besides, I think I might be in love."

Roscoe whined again and started off in the direction of the cave. Wynter ambled behind him happier than she could remember being in a long time.

<h1 style="text-align:center">Chapter Four</h1>

Wynter was back at the clearing early the next morning eager to see Ethan again and even Noah. Roscoe had left in the opposite direction that morning, she assumed to meet with his own friends. They would meet up later that night, but today was all about a little human interaction.

"Wow, you're here early," Ethan observed when he and Noah walked up. Noah was still yawning and clearly opposed to being up that early for anything much less training.

"I'm a morning person," Wynter chirped cheerily.

"Yeah, so this is my brother Noah. Noah this is Wynter," Ethan introduced.

"I know. I know," Noah griped. "She's all you've talked about since yesterday."

Wynter smiled at the unexpected attention, but Ethan turned a lovely shade of red. It was kind of cute on him.

So, Wynter thought optimistically, he has thought about me as much as I have thought about him. That was a flattering and encouraging thought.

"Um...I'm going to go ahead and work with Noah first, because he has to be back home by lunch."

"Ok, I'll just wait over here and watch if that's alright."

"Sure."

As Wynter turned to go sit down, she saw Ethan out of the corner of her eye slap a hand to the back of Noah's head.

"Ow, what was that for?" Noah demanded.

Ethan hissed something under his breath, and Wynter chuckled to herself.

Ethan and Noah worked together for only an hour, and Noah had crushed many, many snowballs. Wynter had lost count somewhere around forty. Noah was obviously frustrated, but Ethan was very patient with him. It was endearing to watch the way he worked with his younger brother. Despite all the sibling rivalry, Ethan's love and concern for Noah was shinning through.

"Ok, get on home," Ethan ordered Noah after the first hour.

"Awe, come on. I haven't levitated even one snowball," Noah whined.

"That's not my fault and neither is you not having any more time. Mom said to practice for an hour then you have to go back home to clean your room."

"I can clean it later."

"That's what got you into this trouble in the first place," Ethan pointed out. "Just go home and clean your room before Mom gets really mad."

"Fine," Noah grumbled as he stomped away.

Ethan reached an arm out for Wynter and helped her up. "I thought he might put up more of a fight, and Mom said that she would hold me responsible if he wasn't back home in an hour."

"You don't have to go home, too, to clean your room? Wynter asked curiously.

"Nah…I'm a little OCD about my bedroom. It drives me nuts if everything isn't in its proper place. Noah is sort of my counterpart. He would never clean his room if he could convince our mom to just close the door and ignore it."

"Oh." Wynter was a little surprised by this revelation. She had thought Ethan was a pretty laid back guy. She definitely liked keeping things tidy and in its proper place, but she wouldn't call herself OCD. That implied that he got a little crazy with it or was some type of germ-a-phobe.

"What about you?"

"Me? I keep things neat and clean, I guess, but I'm not… manic about it."

"Manic," Ethan repeated with a chuckle. "That's actually a good way to put it. Dad says that even as a baby I couldn't stand a mess and that I was cleaning by the time I could walk."

"That is a bit…"

"Extreme, I know. Hey, at least I can admit it. Are you ready to try again?"

"Sure."

"Ok, we'll start with trying to get your eyes open. There's no sense in levitating it higher if you can't even see it, right?"

"I guess not." Wynter didn't see the sense in levitating a snowball at all. It was an impractical use of magic. It was hardly more than a parlor trick for amusement. Did the South Pole people ever use magic for a purpose?

Ethan turned up the snow into a ball and said, "Alright."

"Can I ask you a question?" Wynter wondered.

"Of course, shoot."

"What is the purpose of magic?"

"The purpose?"

"Yeah, I mean why is it so important to learn?"

"Well, there's lots of reasons. It's cool. It's a sign of maturity. Plus it can be useful?"

"How?"

"How what?"

"How can it be useful?"

"Oh, um, my mom uses it when she cooks to keep several pots stirring at once or to get spices from the shelf. My dad uses when he works on the snowmobile or other stuff like that. He can get tools he needs from across the room. Oh and, it works great when you clean up after a blizzard like yesterday! Instead of spending hours shoveling all the walkways, I was able to just move huge chunks of snow at a time using magic."

Wynter nodded thoughtfully. "I see." The South Pole people were highly ineffectual. He had only moved the snow, and he had only moved it chunks at a time. Wynter could have done away completely with the snow that had covered the walkway in a matter of seconds. She would have to be very careful not to get too comfortable and use her magic too well in front of Ethan or Noah for that matter.

Wynter pretended several times to be unsuccessful before she finally levitated the snowball an inch off the ground.

"Yes!" Ethan exclaimed, lifting her right off the ground and swinging her in a circle.

Wow, he got excited easy. How excited would he get if he could see what she really could do? He'd probably get real excited but in a very negative way since that would most certainly give away where she was from and where she was not.

Ethan put her back down. "How do you feel?"

"Great!"

"You up for some more work?"

"Sure."

"Perfect. Let's see if you can get it higher now. Do the exact same thing you did but really focus hard on holding it there longer and getting it up higher."

"Ok."

Wynter levitated the snowball an inch a couple times then moved it up another inch.

"That's it!" Ethan encouraged. "Keep going."

She did. Wynter levitated it time and time again moving up one additional inch at a time until at last she had it at waist height.

"You're doing so great, but I'm sure you could use a break by now. I'm hungry anyway. You want to go to my house for lunch?"

"I'd love to."

"Good, come on." Ethan led the way quickly back to his house.

"Hey, Mom," Ethan called as they walked in the back door into the kitchen. "I invited Wynter over for lunch."

"I hope that's ok," Wynter quickly interjected since Ethan did not seem to be inclined to ask for himself.

"Of course, sweetheart. Come in and get warmed up," Ethan's mom said. She had a cheerful voice and a large smile. Wynter could tell already that she was going to like Ethan's mom.

Ethan had already plopped down in a chair at the table ready to be fed, a typical teenage boy, or so Wynter imagined. "Is there anything I can do to help?"

"Oh, no, everything is just about ready. You go ahead and have a seat at the table. I'm Mrs. Vikki, and Mr. Norm should be down here any minute with Noah." Mrs. Vikki said sweetly.

Ethan nudged the chair next to him, and Wynter assumed that meant he wanted her to sit there next to him. Wynter did sit as Ethan was telling his mom, "She met Noah this morning."

"How is he doing?" Mrs. Vikki inquired.

"Not too bad. He actually levitated a snowball today...a little."

Mrs. Vikki nodded thoughtfully. "And, how are you doing, Wynter?"

"I'm learning...slowly," Wynter answered bashfully. She didn't know why she was being so bashful about the most pathetic show of magic ever, but she was.

"She's great," Ethan added. "She's got the snowball waist high already."

"Yeah, yeah," Noah grumbled as he walked in with a man who remarkably resembled him following in tow.

"Noah," the man said in a warning voice. "You must be Wynter."

"Yes, sir." Wynter could feel herself blushing. The whole family knew her name; she must have been the topic of discussion last night.

"I'm Mr. Norm."

"How's the room coming?" Mrs. Vikki asked Noah.

"It's almost finished," he offered eagerly. "We're using magic!"

"I hope your dad isn't doing it for you."

"Nah," Mr. Norm spoke up. "I figured that while we were at it, I could show him a few things, maybe help him out a little."

"Yeah, it's really cool. Someday when I can do all the things Dad does, I won't ever have a messy room again."

With a knowing grin Mrs. Vikki said, "That's wonderful, but I don't think I'll hold my breath waiting for you to be that organized."

"I will be. Just wait and see." Noah was excited. It was cute to see how excited he was about magic changing his life.

Mrs. Vikki levitated a big pot of stew to the table as well as five bowls, spoons, and napkins.

"I don't want stew," Noah whined.

"Noah, behave. We have company. If you don't want to eat that is entirely up to you, but you will be hungry before supper," Mrs. Vikki scolded.

"Do you like stew?" Noah asked Wynter.

"I do. I love stew." It felt like forever since she had had stew. It felt like forever since she had anything other than meat that Roscoe had hunted down. Wynter had always been one to eat a healthy and balanced diet, but she never realized how much she would miss vegetables until they were gone.

Wynter took a big bite of stew after blowing it generously. Wow, that was real beef, like actual cow. It must have come from a store. You couldn't hunt down cows in this area. Wynter would have to look into getting a job so that she could go to the store. Eventually she would need fruits and vegetables.

"So, Dad, I was telling Mom that I really want a new pair of skis," Ethan mentioned trying hard to sound sly."

"Oh? And, what did your mom say?"

"She said that I couldn't have them until I can buy them myself."

"Then I think that pretty much answered your question."

"Come on. How am I supposed to buy new skis? You know minors can't work."

Oh well, there went the notion of getting a job. No one was going to hire her if she looked sixteen, and producing ID would only out her as a Clause.

"You have birthday money if you didn't spend it all," Mrs. Vikki pointed out.

"I don't have enough left."

"Then you'll have to save up." Mrs. Vikki cleared her throat and asked, "Wynter, do you live close by? Have I met your parents?"

"Oh, um, no. I...I don't think you would know them."

"Oh." Mrs. Vikki looked at Mr. Norm with some sort of unspoken language passing between them.

"Maybe they could come by for a meal sometime."

"They work a lot." There, that wasn't a lie. Her parents did work a lot.

"Oh, that's a shame. Are you alone a lot?"

"Well, I'm really mature for my age, so I basically raise myself at this point."

"Well, you're welcome here anytime. Just drop in whenever you'd like. You have an open invitation."

"Thank you. That's very kind."

"School starts back Monday. Are you going to be there?" Ethan asked none too subtle.

"No, I'm home schooled." That had been the truth once upon a time. There was no need to mention that she had already graduated.

"Too bad. I could have shown you around. I'll be a senior this year."

Noah, who did not want stew, ate two big bowls. He kept Wynter entertained with his enthusiasm for the food that he did not even want. When he stopped whining, Noah was really a cute kid. He had a great sense of humor, and he had the sweetest laugh. Ethan didn't know how lucky he was to have a little brother around even during the annoying times.

Mrs. Vikki and Mr. Norm were great. They were insistent that Wynter could come by anytime she wanted and stay as long as she wanted. She was always welcome at their house. Wynter thought they might be a little suspicious that her parents left her alone too much and were not overall good parents. They did of course, but Ethan's parents did not know how old she really was. Already they were including her in discussions like she was one of the family. It was amazing. She had a real feeling of inclusion, whereas at home she had always felt more like a nuisance than anything else.

"You ever play video games?" Ethan asked after lunch.

"Well yeah," Wynter answered as if it should have been a given. Growing up at the North Pole, the toy capital of the world, she had filled her time with hours of game time.

"Want to play?"

"Sure."

They spent all afternoon playing video games until Mrs. Vikki called them to supper. After only one afternoon, Wynter could tell what type of games Ethan enjoyed most, and she could think of at least ten off the top of her head currently at the North Pole that Ethan would love. That was neither here nor there though since Santa did not deliver toys to the South Pole.

It wasn't that the boys and girls here were necessarily naughty. It was just a byproduct of the North South feud.

Santa wasn't about to deliver toys to the South Pole, and the South Polers were not about to let Santa fly over their territory anyway.

It was sad really. Wynter doubted that anyone could even tell her what all the fuss was about any more, and yet if Mrs. Vikki and Mr. Norm knew where she was really from they wouldn't have been nearly as nice. Ethan and Noah probably wouldn't be very nice either for that matter. For what reason? What made them so different that they couldn't be civil to one another?

Wynter pondered this while she ate supper. The food was delicious, but her thoughts were an endless storm with no solution.

Wynter knew she needed to head back after supper; Roscoe would surely be irritable by now. She said her good-byes and thanked them for their hospitality.

Roscoe was waiting just outside the cave when Wynter returned. He huffed and turned into the cave with Wynter following behind.

"You missed me. Did you have fun today?"

Roscoe nodded his big, shaggy bear head.

"See, then what is there to be upset about? We both had fun, and I did come back. You could have gotten back into the cave at any time you wanted, and you full well know that."

Roscoe curled up at the foot of the bed, tucking his head, and closing his eyes.

"Did you eat?"

Roscoe huffed but didn't so much as open his eyes. Wynter smiled at her irritated polar bear before climbing onto his back and hugging him tight. "I missed you too," she sighed into his fur. "Besides, we'll still have plenty of time to spend together while the boys are in school."

Chapter Five

Wynter quickly fell into a routine of spending her weekdays with Roscoe and her weekends with Ethan and his family.

"When was the first time you went snowboarding?" Noah asked eagerly as they followed Ethan to what he called the perfect snowboarding spot.

"Oh," she had been sixteen, but obviously that wouldn't work since she was only now supposed to be sixteen. "I think I was fourteen," she quickly lied.

"Man, your parents didn't let you have any fun," Noah marveled. The kid really had no idea.

"Don't be rude, Noah. Not everyone has older siblings who can go with them," Ethan pointed out. "Here we are."

Wynter looked around. It was an interesting terrain, bumpy and all downhill. It looked tame enough, though, but looks could be deceiving. Wynter had never been snowboarding when magic didn't play a part in it. Snowboarding with magic could be…intense. Surely she could pull it off here without magic. Although…she really only knew the idea behind it since she had never done it without magic. Deciding to play it safe, Wynter stood back and let the boys go first; that way she could watch them and copy.

Ethan went first so that he would be at the bottom of the hill when Noah got there. Ethan was very athletic. He was all grace and coordination. The way he moved held Wynter captive as if hypnotized. His muscles bunched and stretched, sending him zig-zaging this way and that. He made it all look so easy, but Wynter knew that wasn't true. It took a great deal of balance and concentration.

Noah took off before Ethan reached the bottom of the hill, screaming all the way. Noah was certainly excitable, and Wynter couldn't help but smile at his enthusiasm. Life was one great adventure to Noah, and he lived every second to its fullest. He held nothing back either when it came to his excitement for life.

Wynter pushed off. Unsure what to expect, she was surprised to find that it wasn't too different from snowboarding with magic. She let out an excited,

"Whoooooooo," of her own as wind rushed up to meet her whipping through her hair.

"Whooo-whooooooo," Noah answered her scream, and Wynter couldn't help herself. Before she could take another breath she was screaming again.

Wynter and Noah were speeding down the hill screaming back and forth. Screams echoed off the snow and ice, reverberating all around them, creating a symphony of screams. By now Ethan stood at the bottom of the hill shaking his head, probably at the childishness of it all, but Wynter could not have cared any less. She was having fun…with actual friends. She was excited, and she didn't care who knew it.

All afternoon long the three enjoyed themselves. Noah and Wynter remained vocal the whole day through. Ethan never joined in on the screaming, but Wynter had caught him on several occasions when he thought no one was looking smiling as Wynter or Noah let out a whooping holler. He might have thought he was too cool to scream and carry on, but he still enjoyed the excitement in his own way.

Wynter was still amped up on adrenaline when she returned home that evening. Roscoe was out hunting, and he snorted when her excitedly frenzied footsteps alerted his waiting prey to his presence.

The seal flopped across the ice and dove into the water through a hole in the ice. Roscoe lumbered over to the hole and plopped down in frustration to wait out the seal.

Wynter sat down a safe distance from where the gore was destined to take place and thought back over her day. She would have enjoyed incorporating magic, yet she had more fun boarding with Ethan and Noah than she had ever had alone with her magic. Magic was certainly a special trait to be treasured, but it did not take the place of family and friends. Love was irreplaceable.

Of course, she had not always been alone before she came to the South Pole. Once upon a time her parents had gone boarding with her. That had been back when they were first teaching her how. Once she had the idea, they left her to her own devices. Occasionally a few of the elves would come out on break to watch her for a while; however, they could not stay long. There were always more toys to be made, more gifts to be wrapped, lists to check, maps to be plotted.

The reindeer did not have the same rigorous schedule. Maybe that was a big part of why she had bonded so quickly with Roscoe. She had been used to spending a lot of her time with animals. She and the reindeer went sledding often. It gave them a chance to get out and keep in shape, and it gave Wynter a fun way to pass the time. They never took her dad's sleigh; she knew better than that. She had her own sleigh that she had built herself with the use of magic of course. She would harness the reindeer up, and they would go racing through the woods until they got to Wynter's favorite snowboarding spot. She then would unharness the reindeer and let them roam about while she snowboarded. They would stay out all day before she rounded them all back up and headed back for home.

She did miss the reindeer. She wondered idly if anyone was taking them out for exercise since she had been gone. She hated to think of them cooped up inside the stables all year long until their famous flight. It would be difficult for them to make it all around the world in one night if they had been shut inside eating oats every other day of the year. They needed exercise to stay healthy. It would just be cruel to keep them locked up in their stables all three hundred and sixty-four days a year.

Wynter cringed to think of Blitzen being caged up all year long. She would completely spas out. Blitzen had more excess energy than anyone knew what to do with. If she wasn't given a way to work out all that energy, she would simply go crazy and chew her way out of that stable if she had to. Blitzen had always been a bit hyper and harder to settle down. If she only got to escape her prison once a year, there would be no controlling her.

Santa would be sorry if he didn't get Comet and Dasher some exercise. Their names might imply that they were fast, but the truth was that they were the two slowest on the team. If no one kept up their exercise regiment, Comet and Dasher would definitely slow the team down if they were able to make the run at all. Those two wouldn't mind spending their days lazing about, but it would definitely show when they couldn't pull their own weight on Christmas Eve.

Donner, on the other hand, was wicked fast. No way were Comet and Dasher going to keep up with him if they spend the whole year being lazy. Speaking of Donner, he loved to run. It was his favorite thing in the whole world. If he wasn't given the opportunity to just run all out every so often, it would take a major toll on his spirits, and that wouldn't do anyone any good. He was sort of the leader of the group. He was the oldest, and all the others sort of looked to him for guidance. Wynter knew for a fact that when working as a team, the others would more often than not mimic Donner and match his pace.

Dancer and Prancer loved to spend hours at a time just out in the open. They really came to life surrounded by all that open space to play. You could literally watch their eyes light up as they moved about. Wynter had named them herself. They had amused her so much as fawns. Dancer would literally dance all about. There was simply no other way to describe the way he moved. He would trot around shaking his hind quarters the whole way. He would shimmy and shake all the way across a field of ice.

Prancer pranced. He didn't trot or run around like the others. He would sort of hop from hoof to hoof. He was a happy go lucky prancer. He hopped about like he didn't have a care in the world. It hurt Wynter to think of them being unable to dance and prance to their heart's content like the free spirits they really were at heart.

Poor Cupid and Vixen they craved human love and attention. Wynter's grandfather had actually named Cupid when he was just a newborn. It was uncanny the way he stole everyone's heart right away, so Grandfather said that he was a natural cupid. The name just sort of stuck, but it was true. Cupid had a way of winning over even the coldest of hearts, and he was never happier than when he was having a heart to heart with anyone who cared enough to share. Wynter had sat in the stables next to Cupid and emptied her heart many times. He would watch her so intently like he was really listening and understanding. Like Roscoe, Cupid was a true friend despite the lack of humanity.

Vixen was a cuddler. She was always cuddling up to anyone who ventured close enough. She also had a tight bond with Santa even though Daddy really didn't spend all that much time with her. Mom used to playfully call her a vixen, flirting shamelessly with her husband. Ironically enough the name stuck so strongly that no one can even remember what her name had originally been. She was great when you needed a hug. Vixen was never too busy to give a hug or just cuddle when you were feeling blue.

In some ways that eight reindeer team had been more of a family to Wynter than her own parents. Sad. Now she lived with a polar bear. Was there something about Wynter that rejected human affection?

"You up for a game of dodge ball?" Ethan asked Wynter and Noah.

"No way! That's not fair. You can throw snowballs with magic. Wynter can't throw them yet, and I can only levitate them a little bit," Noah rejected.

"Snowballs?" Wynter questioned.

"Yeah, we play dodge ball with snowballs. It's fun. Want to try?"

"I told you it isn't fair."

"What do you want to do then?"

"Tag," Noah announced proudly. "I'm a really fast runner," he added for Wynter's benefit.

Ethan studied Noah for a second before suggesting, "How about both. We can play freeze tag and dodge ball at the same time. No hitting someone with a snowball while they are frozen. After you're tagged, you have to stay frozen while you count to thirty."

"That's too high. I don't like counting that long."

"Fine, you have to count to fifteen then, and to even out the odds, you and Wynter will be a team."

Noah looked at Wynter. Wynter looked at Noah. With a mischievous grin they both said, "Agreed," and took off running.

Ethan sent the first snowball flying at Noah's back, but Noah glanced over his shoulder at the last second and made a sharp turn to the right. Wynter swirled together a snowball and levitated to her hands. She let it fly towards Ethan, but her aim without magic left much to be desired. The snowball flew too far left and high. Ethan didn't even have to make a move to dodge the snowball.

"Smooth, Wynter. Real smooth," he teased. He focused his attention on Wynter as he sent his second snowball sailing toward her. He was smiling in her direction, and Wynter was so distracted that she almost forgot to dodge.

Nevertheless, Wynter ducked the snowball easily at the last second but had to take off running as soon as she popped back up, because Ethan was already hot on her tail. He was no slowpoke, but Wynter had spent all her life running with reindeers. He never stood a chance of catching her, but while his attention was on Wynter, Noah was behind Ethan and quickly eating up the space between them.

Just as Ethan had a snowball levitated and taking aim, Noah tagged his back and screamed, "Freeze, sucker!"

Wynter couldn't help but laugh at how easily they had gotten Ethan first. "Come on," she called to Noah. They ducked behind a large chunk of ice for cover, and Wynter began swirling together snowballs as fast as she could only making one at a time.

She could have not only built a more formidable fort but also formed many more snowballs at one time, but the game was already two on one. They didn't want to make it too unfair for Ethan.

Noah picked up the snowballs and began lobbing them at Ethan as fast as his arms could work. Fifteen seconds did not keep Ethan frozen in his tracks for long, and Ethan was more interested in offence than defense.

He ran through the barrage of snowballs, getting hit more than a couple of times, pushing his way toward where Wynter and Noah were holed up. "We've got to move," Noah squealed with an excited grin.

They grabbed what snowballs they could and started running. A rather large snowball pummeled Noah from behind. Noah staggered a little but managed to stay on his feet and continue running. He glanced over his shoulder and huffed, "Get down, Wynter!"

Wynter ducked just in time to feel the wind from a snowball brush through her hair on the top of her head. Unfortunately, she was not nearly as coordinated as Noah, and when she began to stumble she couldn't right herself again. Wynter went down face first in a heap of tangled legs. She was giggling too much to accomplish much else.

"I'll come back for you," Noah promised as he screamed over his shoulder.

By the time Wynter rolled over to her back, Ethan was there waiting on her. He was hovering over her, his face only inches from her own. His grey eyes were lined up with her own. They looked like grey storm clouds rolling. Wynter was too taken by his amazing eyes to take in what else Ethan was doing. "Gotcha'," he said and tagged her shoulder. Then he was up and running again, going after Noah.

Wynter counted to fifteen and got back to her feet ready to rejoin the fray. Except now she found herself standing between the two brothers. This was what she imagined a regular game of dodge ball would look like if she were dealing with two against one odds.

Noah knelt to the ground and started forming a large snowball with his hands since this proved faster for him than using magic. While Noah was preoccupied, Ethan let a snowball fly at Wynter. She dodged it easily, but there was already another coming at her. She dodged again with more difficulty this time.

"Get down!" Noah warned.

Wynter dropped to the ground just in time for a melon sized snowball to wiz over her head. Ethan dodged easily, and Wynter looked back to see Noah struggling to make a second snowball. Wynter formed a snowball right in front of Noah's busy hands.

With a grin, he stopped the one he had been working on. "Thanks," he said picking up the snowball and sending it sailing. Wynter focused on making one snowball at a time for Noah to use as arsenal since her own aim left so much to be desired.

"He's coming for you," came Noah's breathless warning as he continued to throw snowballs as quickly as possible.

Wynter began a slow crawl towards Noah. She was trying to stay as low as possible so to stay out of the way of flying snowballs from both sides. All the while she continued the outpouring of snowballs to keep Noah on the attack. She knew that Ethan had to be gaining on her rapidly.

Suddenly she was tackled from behind and rolled onto her back. Ethan had her arms and legs pinned to the cold ground with his own. "You're getting faster," he grinned.

Wynter knew she needed to be more careful with her displays of magic, but with Ethan grinning down at her like that, she couldn't find the enthusiasm to care. His grin was so infectious, it made Wynter grin in return despite the cold seeping through her clothes.

Just then a snowball crashed into the top of Ethan's head. It shattered and sprinkled ice and water onto Wynter's face. She sputtered and tried shaking the ice off since Ethan still had her arms pinned.

"Leave Wynter alone, and come after someone your own size," Noah demanded loudly.

With a wicked grin, Ethan sprang from his crouch freeing Wynter's arms and legs. "Someone like you, half pint?" he responded.

Ethan tackled Noah and both boys began rolling around on the snow and ice wrestling and wearing over enthused smiles.

Wynter sat up to watch as she counted to fifteen. Ethan had essentially tagged her after all. On fifteen, Wynter popped up and brought a snowball to her hand. The boys were moving so quickly back and forth, she had trouble deciding where to aim it, but Wynter threw the snowball anyway. It missed. Luckily it missed them both. She would have felt bad if she had hit her own teammate.

She brought another to her hand as they moved closer. Again the snowball missed, but Wynter continued to advance on the two boys who were too preoccupied to notice. She continued to throw one snowball after another until she was so close to the boys there was no way she could miss.

"Hey!" Ethan called as he realized he was being bombarded with snowballs. He pushed to his feet ready to retreat, but Noah tagged his calf instead calling out, "Freeze. Get him Wynter!"

She brought to hand this time a very slushy snowball and walked around to face Ethan. "Don't," Ethan said just as Wynter smashed the slushy mess into his face.

Wynter took off in a mad dash to get away, knowing that his fifteen seconds had to be coming to a close soon. She wasn't fast enough, though. Ethan grabbed the back of Wynter's jacket and pulled her back. Her feet went out from under her, and she landed roughly with her back against Ethan's front. He held his ground, keeping them upright, but then with a loud "Omph" Noah tackled from behind sending them all three to the ice cold ground.

Rolling around, they all three vied for the upper hand until Ethan called a stop to the fun and games. "Ok, ok, ok. The half pint still has homework to get done, and the sun is beginning to set."

"Awe, come on," Noah whined.

"No, you know how peeved Mom will be if we miss super. Don't make it worse by working on homework late into the night."

Noah conceded to the truth of Ethan's point, and they all said their good byes.

Chapter Six

In her free time Wynter began to experiment with different hobbies. Her favorite by far was photography. There was so much beauty to be captured in the South Pole. What other photographer could get as close to a living, breathing polar bear as she could? She got some amazing close ups of Roscoe and even a few really great ones during a hunt. Not too many people would be crazy enough to get close to a hunting polar, but Wynter knew that she had nothing to fear.

Those of the hunt had been some of her favorites. She much preferred it when her subjects were completely unaware that she was taking their picture. It made the pictures more realistic and more believable.

There was also so much more she could do with the photos using magic rather than a dark room or even a computer. She could develop her pictures in a snap, resizing them as many times as she wanted until she found the perfect size to suit her. What may take others hours on the computer, Wynter could do in minutes. All she had to do was envision the changes she wished to make then make it happen.

Of course Ethan and his family didn't know this. They thought she put in hours of work when she wasn't busy with her own school work. Wynter felt a little guilty about all the lies between her and the family that she was quickly coming to think of as her own extended family, but she knew if she came clean she would feel far worse. The last thing she wanted was to lose her new family, but that was precisely what would happen if they were ever to find out who or what she really was. Wynter did not want to believe that. She liked to think if they ever found her out, they would forgive her for lying and love her despite her origins, but deep down she knew that was farfetched. She preferred to live in ignorant bliss never testing the waters.

Ethan and Noah turned out to be willing and good natured models for Wynter's photographs. Wynter had so many photos of them she had enough to start a gallery of each of them, not that Wynter had any interests in opening a gallery. Her photography was something just for her that she enjoyed doing.

One particular photo had been snapped during a rare tender moment between Ethan and Noah. It had been during one of Noah's magic lessons. Both boys were looking each other in the face as they talked. Wynter had sat quietly to the side snapping pictures. In her favorite picture, both boys' faces were lit up with love as they gazed at one another. Wynter knew at once that that would be a nearly impossible photo to ever recreate.

Wynter blurred the background and left only Ethan and Noah themselves crystal clear within the photo. She put the emphasis on the boys' shinning faces then enlarged the picture onto a canvas that she then framed and hung above the head of her bed. There were other photos scattered across the cave of Noah and Ethan as well as their parents and Roscoe. There were even landscape and other wildlife photos, but that one hanging above her bed was above and beyond Wynter's favorite of all time.

Noah sat one afternoon looking through a stack of Wynter's more recent photos. "Hey, why don't you ever take any pictures of us with the wildlife?" he asked.

"Because, then it wouldn't be wild," Ethan answered for her.

"Sure it would."

"I don't think that animals tame enough to interact with humans would be considered wild," Ethan pointed out.

"We could feed the wild animals. Then she could take our picture with the wildlife."

"Yeah, and maybe the wildlife would eat you, idiot."

"Well, I think it's a good idea. Come on, Wynter." Noah started gathering food from the fridge and pantry and dropping it into a plastic bag.

"I don't think this is a good idea, Noah," Ethan chimed in.

"I didn't ask you," Noah retorted as he walked out the door undeterred.

Wynter followed behind Noah determined not to let any harm come to him. She loved him like he was her own brother, and she would rather out herself than let Noah get hurt. She had seen him like this before, though. When Noah got something into his head, just about the only way to stop him was to tie him up. He was head strong to say the least and fearless.

Ethan was right on Wynter's tail, trying desperately to stop his younger brother from doing something completely stupid.

"Shut up or go home," Noah snipped. "You're going to scare away any animals."

As it turned out Noah did not need as much protection as either Wynter or Ethan had suspected. Noah stopped about one hundred yards from a colony of penguins and pulled out a can of sardines from his bag. He took the sardines from the can and inched closer inch by inch until he had cut the distance in half. Then he sat down in the snow with his arms propped on his legs palms up filled with sardines.

"What is he doing?" Ethan whispered next to my ear.

Wynter shook her head at a loss. Noah was still a good fifty yards from the penguins. What did he intend to accomplish?

Noah sat there nearly thirty minutes before he caught the attention of the first penguin. Over the next half hour penguins sniffed the air and watched Noah curiously. Noah sat unmoving watching the penguins watch him.

Wynter had never seen Noah show so much patience for anything. Wynter and Ethan sat down side by side and watched Noah as he patiently watched the penguins. Another hour passed before the first penguin cautiously approached Noah.

It inched closer watching Noah meticulously. When Noah still failed to even so much as flinch, the penguin moved forward to his hand. The penguin watched the sardines in Noah's hand and watched Noah for a few more minutes before taking a tentative bite of sardine.

By that point Wynter was already clicking away. She had brought the camera up and had started snapping pictures as soon as the lone penguin had started advancing closer to Noah.

When the first penguin began to eat from Noah's hand a second joined in and a third, and so it continued until the sardines were completely gone. As the penguins realized that Noah had nothing more to offer them, they waddled back to their original starting point. After all the penguins had abandoned him, Noah slowly stood and moved carefully back over to Wynter and his brother.

"Did you get it? Did you get the pictures?" Noah asked eagerly.

"I did. That was amazing."

"How did you do that?" Ethan asked.

"The penguins were hungry," Noah said with a shrug. "All I had to do was show them that I wasn't going to hurt them."

"Wow."

"Can I see them?" Noah asked.

"Not yet," Wynter replied slyly. "Let me clean them up, and I'll bring them by tomorrow for you to see."

"Uhhhgggh, I don't want to wait for tomorrow," Noah whined.

"You just waited almost an hour and a half for penguins to eat out of your hand, but you don't want to wait a day to see the pictures?" Ethan asked.

"That was different. They were scared. Wynter's not scared of me."

"Which is why I won't give in no matter how much you try," Wynter smiled.

"That's not fair."

"Come on. Let's go home," Ethan instructed turning away. "See you tomorrow, Wynter," he called back over his shoulder.

Noah stomped behind him letting his disappointment be known.

As Wynter started back for her cave, she got an eerie feeling that she was being watched. Quickly looking around, she couldn't see anyone, but she remained vigilant until finally returning home to her nice warm cave.

Thankfully the eerie feeling had passed before Wynter got to the cave. She had lost whoever was watching her, if there had been anyone to begin with. She hadn't met many of the residence of the South Pole, but even though none of them would risk exposing her to the regular humans, she had no doubt that they would have no qualms about exposing her to Ethan's family.

The pictures were fun to work with, but it was one of the first few that she had taken that had ended up the best in her opinion. Before any of the other penguins had waddled over to check out Noah and his sardines for themselves, just one penguin stood in front of where Noah sat eating from his hand. Surrounded by the icy landscape, Noah and the penguin stood out in bright contrast. From the outside looking in, it appeared that Noah and the penguin were completely in tune with one another. It was like he was the penguin whisperer.

The picture had a magic all its own, and Wynter knew from the moment she saw it that it was something special. She enlarged and framed it for Noah, certain that he would love it. The next day, however, Noah surprised her.

"Oh my!" Mrs. Vikki exclaimed. "That is breathtaking. Noah, I can't believe you did that."

"Yeah, the picture is great, but I wish you all could have been as close as I was. It was way cooler in real life. The penguin really trusted me, you know, and his little beak kept poking my hand when he ate."

"So, you don't like the picture?" Wynter inquired as Ethan and Mr. Norm continued to flip through the other pictures.

"I love the picture! The picture is awesome! It's just that being there and actually feeding them was awesome too. I wish you could have done it too."

"I don't think I have the talent you do."

"What talent?" Noah wondered honestly baffled.

"The way you were with those penguins yesterday," Ethan spoke up, "that was definitely a talent. Maybe you could do wildlife research or something like that someday."

"Or maybe I'd like to be a ranger," Noah inserted slyly gauging everyone's reaction. South Pole rangers were over more than just the wildlife. They were almost like a homeland security. It was their job to make sure that the human South Pole researchers didn't stumble onto more information about the South Polers than they wanted them to have.

Everyone continued to marvel at the pictures; they didn't say anything about Noah's remark about becoming a ranger. Wynter gave him a grin and conspiratorial wink.

"Hey, Mom, do you have any fish I could take?" Noah asked.

"Whatever for?"

"To feed to the animals."

"Oh, honey, I don't know..."

"You just said it was breathtaking."

"I know, and it is. I'm just not so sure it's safe." Mrs. Vikki looked to Mr. Norm for help.

"Oh, um..."

"Come on, Dad. It was the coolest thing ever, and I was extra careful. Wasn't I, Ethan?"

"Yeah, I was shocked at how slow, deliberate, and patient he was," Ethan admitted.

"Well, ok, but you have to have Ethan with you, and Ethan, I want you to take a gun along just to be on the safe side."

Ethan nodded while Noah ran out of the room whooping and hollering the whole way to the kitchen to find some fish.

Wynter didn't mention to anyone that the gun was unnecessary. If anything happened, Ethan wouldn't have time to aim the gun before the animal or animals were exploding from the inside out. Violent? Perhaps, but that was the risk the animals took if they crossed the people that Wynter loved.

Ethan and Wynter had expected Noah to seek out another colony of penguins, but that was not the case.

Noah stopped just short of a hole in the ice. Wynter recognized the ripples in the water as a sign that a seal had recently dove underneath. Noah must have recognized the signs too, because he sat down and started to unwrap the fish.

"Oh no, uh-uh, no way," Ethan reacted.

"Noah, seals can be very violent. I don't think this is a very good idea," Wynter reasoned.

"I think it is a very good idea."

"Not a chance," Ethan challenged.

"You can back up if you're scared."

"We're scared for you," Wynter admonished. "Backing up won't help solve anything."

"Course it will. You're scaring the seal. If you would back up and shut up it might not come up fighting because of lack of choice when it runs out of air."

"You said might," Ethan pointed out.

"Yep, but it definitely will if you don't back up and shut up."

Wynter spotted Roscoe across the icy plain peeking out from behind a glacier. She knew in her heart that Roscoe wouldn't let harm come to the people she loved anymore than she would. She was not above using magic to save Noah's life either. She wrapped her hands around Ethan's arm and gently pulled him back.

"I don't like this," Ethan protested.

"I know," Wynter said with a pat on his arm. When they were back adequately, Ethan raised the gun and kept it trained on the opening in the ice.

Noah sat the fish on the ice in front of him and waited. It didn't take the seal as long as it had the penguin, probably because the seal needed air. He poked up just his snout into the air at first. After a couple of sniffs he raised his head up and peered out over the ice. Noah remained perfectly still as the two sized each other up.

After a while the seal leapt up onto the ice and hesitated to see Noah's reaction, but Noah did not react at all. He remained perfectly still and silent, the very picture of patience and serenity.

The seal had a mixture of colors on its fur. Brown, blonde, and black, his coloring resembled that of an African wild dog. He wasn't overly large or blubberous, so he must have still been a relatively young seal. With no mother seal lurking anywhere nearby, Wynter assumed that the seal had only recently embarked on his own or had been orphaned at a young age.

The seal flopped on its fins closer and closer until it was standing directly in front of Noah. There were a very tense few minutes when Noah and the seal were staring into one another's eyes without backing down.

Wynter barely stifled a gasp when the seal opened its mouth wide revealing sharp teeth designed perfectly for ripping and tearing flesh. Wynter didn't know what held Ethan's trigger finger, but something did.

The seal leaned his head down and clasped the fish inside his powerful jaw. Then the seal proceeded to eat the fish right there standing in front of Noah. Noah continued to sit perfectly still and what appeared to be perfectly at ease. He watched the seal until it had completely devoured the fish.

The seal let out one loud bark before turning and flopping back into the water. Perhaps that was the seal's way of thanking Noah. Whatever had just happened, it was outside the realm of ordinary. Noah had a gift, one that Wynter would call a magical gift.

Noah stood back up and walked back to where Ethan and Wynter stood. "That was totally awesome. Did you see that?"

"See it? I almost shot it?" Ethan replied.

"Why didn't you?" Wynter wondered.

"I don't know."

"I'm glad you didn't. It was only a baby seal, you know," Noah pointed out.

"Where there is a baby seal, there is a mother seal. Let's get out of here," Ethan suggested.

"Fine by me, but I don't think the mommy seal is anywhere to be found," Noah agreed.

"Why do you say that?" Wynter asked.

"If the mommy seal was here, she would have already shown her face. She would have approached instead of allowing her baby to do something so dangerous. Besides there's no other visible holes; the mommy couldn't have held her breath for all that time."

Wynter and Ethan silently accepted his response. It made sense after all.

"Did you get any good pictures?" Noah asked.

"I did."

"Cool. Will you bring them by tomorrow?"

"I can if you'd like."

Noah nodded thoughtfully. "I'd like that. I wonder what other kind of animals I could get close to. Maybe I could get close enough to bond with some of them, you know, make friends. That baby seal looked like he was all alone."

Wynter smiled, because a bond between Noah and that baby seal sounded far too similar to her bond with Roscoe.

Ethan, however, scowled. "Or, maybe Mom and Dad will kill us both when they see the pictures tomorrow."

"Why? Nothing bad happened."

"That's not the point. It could have. You're playing with fire here."

"No…I'm playing with natural predators."

"Right, because that sounds so much better," Ethan interjected as he led them all away until they split ways for their own homes.

Wynter knew instinctively which photo would no doubt be Noah's favorite. She had captured that moment when the seal had opened his mouth but before he began to lower his head toward the fish.

It looked intimidating like the seal was trying to scare Noah away or had been on the start of an attack. Despite the fact that the seal at the very second looked terrifyingly vicious, Noah was still calm, cool, and collected. His face was impassive as he stared forward at the seal and its teeth of doom. The photo gave Noah a daring and courageous look even though in actuality, he had never been threatened or attacked. If you looked closely you could see Roscoe looking on in the background. Roscoe was looking out for Noah, but of course, no one else would know that. Roscoe's presence would only add to the appeal of danger. Noah was bound to find that picture the coolest out of the bunch.

Wynter also knew instinctively that she would have to give that picture to Noah in private. Ethan was right. Their parents would freak out if they had seen what really went down. They were certain to be frantic enough as it was. Seeing that picture would only give them cause to lock the boys away inside for their own protection.

<h1 style="text-align:center">Chapter Seven</h1>

Just as predicted, Mrs. Vikki and Mr. Norm were greatly disturbed by the tale. After that Mrs. Vikki gave Wynter and the boys a list of nice safe outdoor activities they could try. Among the list were building snow critters, freezing bubbles, and snow art.

Building snow critters required imagination and concentration, but it was a little tame after their last activities of watching Noah feed dangerous wildlife.

Noah built a six foot long caterpillar. It looked like a huge snake complete with fangs that had just finished ingesting a meal that had not yet begun to digest, pushing oddly against the snake's pliable body.

Ethan attempted to build a snow horse which didn't resemble anything at all except for a huge mound of shapeless snow.

Wynter was sure their first mistake had been in choosing animals that they were not entirely familiar with. Wynter closed her eyes and pictured clearly in her mind the seal that had eaten Noah's proffered fish.

Next Wynter started by building up a large densely packed mound of snow. She then began carving away pieces until all that was left was the image of the seal in her mind. Ethan sat quietly behind her and watched as the seal took form.

"Well, what do you think?" Wynter asked when she had finished.

"It looks just like him. You're an artist."

"Thank you."

"Hey, Noah, check it out."

Noah turned from what he was doing and peered at Wynter's snow seal. "Oh yeah, it's a seal. Good job, Wynter." Then he went back to his playing.

"Everyone is a critic," Wynter said with a chuckle.

"I can't believe he didn't recognize it," Ethan admonished.

"Do you?"

"Yeah, it's the seal that Noah fed. I saw the picture you gave him by the way. It's good. It's terrifying and heroic all in one. Even I am impressed with how brave the half pint was."

"That is a feat."

"Yeah, I knew you had a knack for pictures, but you can sculpt too," Ethan said pointing to the snow seal.

"Who knew?" Wynter shrugged. She had to admit she had certainly improved since her earlier attempt at creating a snow replica of Roscoe.

Ethan stood and looked Wynter right in the eyes with a smile. His eyes were searching hers…for something. Wynter didn't know what he was looking for, but she hoped more than anything that he found it. It seemed lately that she and Ethan had been firmly rooted in the friend zone. It was wonderful having friends at last. Wynter was grateful for their friendship, but she longed for so much more from Ethan. She looked back at him hoping to see her own emotions reflected back in his eyes.

"Ethan, I'm hungry. Is it almost time for super?" Noah interrupted.

Ethan glanced at his watch and replied, "Yeah, it is. We should get back home." He gave Wynter one more smile then followed Noah away. The moment was over. Whatever Ethan had been looking for would have to wait for another day.

Next on Mrs. Vikki's agenda were freezing bubbles. It was no challenge and rather mundane although pretty, but it did amuse Noah for a while.

They took with them regular bubble solution and wands, but blowing bubbles outside in the freezing South Pole temperatures caused the bubbles to freeze in midair before falling like a weight down to the ground where they promptly shattered into millions of soapy ice shards.

This activity, while fun, could only capture a young boy's attention for a little while. After losing interest they had magic lessons and practiced longer than usual. They had been getting in a lot of extra practice since Mrs. Vikki and Mr. Norm had cracked down on dangerous activities.

The extra practice was really paying off. Noah was really making progress fast. He was easily forming and levitating snowballs now. Wynter had progressed herself to magically throwing snowballs which had drastically improved her aim, but she was scared to reveal much more.

Snow art held more appeal for Noah than the two older ones. They took with them spray bottles full of water and food coloring. Then they were to spray the snow effectively painting the snow and creating their art.

Ethan and Wynter sat down side by side while Noah had a ball painting the snow.

"It has a very Jackson Pollok feel to it," Ethan commented.

"Mmm."

"I thought this would be right up your alley being art and all."

"I lean more towards the less abstract," Wynter admitted.

"Me too." Ethan watched Noah in silence for a few minutes. "I think he should stick to the wildlife."

"I thought your parents put a stop to that."

"They tried. He's been sneaking out the last few nights."

"What!?" Wynter exclaimed.

"Yeah, I didn't like it much either. I tried to talk to him about it. He assured me that he was only watching. He wasn't approaching any of the animals. He said because, and I'm quoting him here 'Mom would notice the missing food.' I guess the danger involved doesn't mean much to him."

"I guess not."

"It's funny. None of us realized how much he liked animals before all this."

"Really?"

"Well, it's not like I hung out all that much with my baby brother before. Now I can't shake him."

"Why is that?"

"He likes you. I think you are his favorite person in the world now. One night he tried to convince my parents to trade me for you so that you could be his sister."

"Awe, that's sweet."

"Unless you're the one he's trying to get rid of."

"He loves you too."

"Yeah, still loves you more, though," Ethan said wrapping his arm around Wynter's shoulders and pulling her into his side. It was warmer there, and they sat like that until Noah had finished his fun, painting in the snow.

It was a possessive sort of embrace, a little less friendly than usual, or maybe that was all in Wynter's imagination. It could have been a little wishful thinking on her part, but either way she was scared to move even a little for fear that Ethan would let her go.

"Hey, Wynter and me are getting better," Noah announced that day during his magic lesson.

"Yeah, so?" Ethan replied.

"Maybe it's time we challenged you to a snowball fight."

"Anytime you're ready, half pint," Ethan laughed.

"Not today. We have to have time to build our fort."

"What kind of fort?" Wynter interjected.

"The big kind that takes a really long time to build."

"Sounds like fun," Wynter agreed.

"I'm game," Ethan said.

"How about in two weeks?" Noah suggested.

"That's a long time. Think you can wait that long?" Ethan taunted.

"You're just scared."

Wynter giggled, and Ethan scowled in her direction. "We'll see who's scared," he boasted.

Noah had an extraordinary work ethic when he was excited about something, and he was excited about the challenge he had presented. Most days they only got to work for a short amount of time due to school, but they were making remarkable progress.

Noah brought with him each day a rectangular shaped plastic box from home that he had dumped hot wheels out of. They used the box as a mold and worked diligently making snow bricks. Next they laid the bricks out in a circular pattern with a gap left out for entry. It took only a week for them to get the fort waist high, and Wynter thought surely Noah would be satisfied, but Noah did not fail to surprise.

He pushed on throughout the next week using a step stool when necessary until the fort was easily taller than both of them. The fort was finally finished with only two days to spare, but Noah didn't waist those last two days. With the remaining prep time, they began forming snowball and storing them inside the fort to have on hand ready for the battle.

While Noah was taking the whole thing very seriously, Ethan was not. Ethan pushed the snow together to build up a clump of snow that he could hide behind. It was taller than Ethan so that he wouldn't have to crouch to hide behind it, but while Noah and Wynter's was an entire circular structure that they could run inside, Ethan's was one massive strait wall. It would be easy to come up behind him in an ambush when he was busy defending himself from the front, something Noah was quick to point out with a wicked grin.

The day of the battle, the three friends met halfway between the two respective forts. Noah insisted they each shake hands, because according to him that was the way it had to be. Ethan, who had apparently seen too many westerns, suggested that they turn and together take ten paces apart then turn and start throwing, so they did.

"One... two... three... four...f ive... six... seven... eight... nine... ten!"

Ethan's first snowball got Noah in the shoulder, but he was unable to throw a second right away. Both Noah and Wynter hit Ethan right in the face with their first throw. As Ethan brushed snow from his face, Noah and Wynter retreated to their fort.

"His fort isn't very strong. It won't hold for long," Noah pointed out. "He doesn't trust your aim, and you've got the most force behind yours since you're using magic. When we go back out, I'll keep Ethan distracted; you keep hitting his fort until it crumbles."

Wynter smiled and nodded, "Ok." There was so much more to Noah than anyone gave him credit for. His abilities with wildlife had come as a surprise to everyone and rightly so, but had no one ever noticed how intelligent he is or how much of a natural born leader he was?

"Let's go!"

Noah tore out of the fort and almost immediately found Ethan who had been trying to sneak up on them. Noah began hitting him with snowball after snowball. He might not have been using magic to throw them, but he had a fair amount of force behind each throw. Noah was one strong kid.

Wynter stood next to Noah and lined her body up so that it would look like she was aiming for Ethan, but every snowball she sent flying went sailing over his head. They hit his fort with a thwack before crumbling and falling to the ground; however, with each ball that tumbled to the ground a little piece of Ethan's fort fell too.

Wynter had only made a small dent in Ethan's fort when she heard an "Ugh" from beside her. She glanced over to see Noah double over holding his stomach where snow still clung to his coat. Wynter sent a snowball in Ethan's direction as she asked Noah, "Are you alright?"

"I'm fine. Get him!"

Wynter laughed as they both started pummeling Ethan with snowballs. Ducking his head, Ethan made a retreat for his fort. Wynter and Noah ran for their own fort to regroup.

"I thought his fort would come down easier than that," Noah admitted forlornly.

"We still got the upper hand," Wynter pointed out.

"Yeah, we got him pretty good. Did you see him running?"

Wynter laughed at Noah's enthusiasm.

"Do you want me to try hitting his fort for a while?"

"Nah, I think I've almost got it," Wynter said. That wasn't entirely the truth. If she were to continue to hit it the way she had been it would have taken forever. That didn't mean she couldn't take it down quickly though. She just had to use a little more magic when no one was looking. "You just keep him distracted and leave the fort to me."

Noah gave one crisp, short nod. He was all business at that point. "Ready?"

"Ready."

They went back on the attack, but Ethan was still hiding behind his fort wall. Noah and Wynter both worked to beat his wall down with the force of their snowballs while Noah taunted his brother.

"Are you ready to surrender already?" Noah asked with a snicker. "We're just getting started."

"So am I."

"So come out and fight then…unless you're scared of the odds. You are outnumbered."

"I'm only outnumbered by amateurs."

"If you say so, but it looks like the amateurs are winning…especially when you start hiding."

It was funny how Noah knew all the right buttons to push. Ethan came charging out ready to fight. Now that

Noah had Ethan doing exactly what he wanted him to do, Noah turned all his attention on Ethan. He was forming snowballs and levitating them up to his hand much quicker than Wynter had ever seen him do. Had the kid been holding back during his lessons in anticipation of a snowball fight?

Noah was throwing the snowballs as hard and as fast as he could. As soon as he would throw one, he had another already on its way to his hand. He and Ethan were pretty evenly matched even though Ethan was using purely magic. What Noah lacked in magic skill, he made up for in brute strength. The kid was a force to be reckoned with.

While Ethan and Noah focused in on bettering one another, Wynter turned her attention on Ethan's wall. With no one looking, she upped her game. She formed larger snowballs and launched them with more force. She could have sent Ethan's wall crashing to the ground without the use of the snowballs at all, but that would have been a bit too noticeable. Neither of the boys seemed to notice the larger balls or greater velocity however.

Suddenly Wynter got that eerie feeling of being watched again. She looked around curiously, but when she didn't see anyone else, she took a slower, more cautious look. She still saw no one watching. It could have been her imagination. After all, Ethan and Noah didn't seem to notice anything amiss. They were still battling away unworried with their surroundings.

Wynter went back to work on bringing down Ethan's wall, but she kept her eyes and ears open for anything out of the ordinary.

"What!?" Ethan cried out as his fort wall finally collapsed to the ground. It was half as tall now, barely up to Ethan's waist. He gave Wynter a cockeyed grin and retreated to crouch behind his half wall.

Noah started in a sprint for their fort, and Wynter followed behind him.

"He's going to be watching us more carefully now."

"Yeah, he knows I did that on purpose."

"Did you see the look on his face? You totally surprised him."

"He won't underestimate me again, though," Wynter pointed out.

"He probably won't underestimate either of us again. I bet he's sorry he agreed to take us on two against one now."

"I bet so," Wynter laughed. The smile on Noah's face was priceless. It made all the hard work from the last couple weeks building that fort worth it. The smile he wore was a combination of pride, sinister, and revenge. Wynter could see now that Noah's challenge had not been a spur of the moment thing. He had been planning this for some time. It was touching that Noah had counted her on his side.

"Ok, when we go back out. I'll go right, and you go left. Stay close to the fort, and we'll hit him from here when he comes back out. We can duck back around the fort wall to avoid getting hit by his snowballs."

"Alright." Wynter wasn't about to argue with him. This was Noah's thing. He had planned it out and obviously had strategies galore stored away in his mind. Not to mention, he was easily besting Ethan thus far. Noah was proving that he was the warrior of the family, fearless, intelligent, patient, and strong.

For some time they stood on either side of the fort hitting Ethan with an endless barrage of snowballs. Ethan was really taking a beating, but for some reason he refused to retreat. Wynter couldn't fathom what was going through his mind. Did he realize already that he wasn't going to win? If so why not surrender instead of taking it like he was?

At last Ethan turned and ducked behind his wall. Wynter let out a sigh of relief. Ethan was no doubt going to be battered and bruised by the end of this game.

"Wynter," Noah called from inside the fort. Wynter slipped inside to see what Noah had planned next.

"Teenage boys are always distracted by pretty girls, so you distract him this time."

Wynter could feel her face flush, but whether at the compliment or the idea that she could distract Ethan she didn't know. "Awe, Noah, do you think I'm pretty?" she teased.

"Everybody thinks you're pretty," Noah said matter of factly. "You will go after Ethan to serve as a distraction while I go around and come up behind him. When he's surrounded on both sides of his fort, he doesn't stand a chance."

"Ready when you are," Wynter agreed still smiling at Noah's kind words.

"Let's go."

Wynter left out of the fort to go after Ethan while Noah hung back to wait for the coast to clear. Wynter had made it nearly half way before Ethan stuck his head out and asked, "Where's Noah?"

"In the fort."

Noah eased around the side of the fort and let loose another snowball to reinforce what Wynter had said.

"What are you doing?" Ethan asked.

"Noah and I thought we would work in shifts for a while since we obviously have the upper hand."

"You think so?"

"Yeah, and I have the first shift, so are you coming out or not?"

"Now why would I fall for that?"

"Fall for what?"

"You want me to come out in the open, because your aim sucks," Ethan retorted.

"I thought I was getting better," Wynter said with a mock pout. "I knocked down your fort."

"Yeah, real hard," Ethan said sarcastically. "You hit a large, stationary wall."

"If you're so sure I can't hit you, why don't you come out and let me try?"

"Are you trying to goad me, Wynter?"

"That depends. Is it working?"

"Nope."

"I could always come back there. It's not a very sophisticated fort, is it?"

"You could try."

"You wouldn't hurt a girl, would you?"

"Want to come back here and find out?"

"Not particularly."

"Why don't you go ahead and admit you're scared, Wynter?"

"Why don't you?"

"Cause I'm not scared." Ethan stood up and launched a snowball right at Wynter.

Unintentionally Wynter let out a very girlified shriek before she ducked out of the way of the snowball. She came up sending a snowball of her own, but it was too late. Ethan had already ducked back below his wall.

"No, you don't sound scared at all, Wynter," he teased.

Without making a sound Wynter crept slowly up to Ethan's wall. She stood up directly in front of where he had popped up the last time.

"What are you waiting on, Wynter?" Ethan called loudly. He obviously didn't know that Wynter had closed the distance behind him, and he was still crouched in the same spot.

Wynter held a snowball in hand ready and waiting. As soon as Ethan popped up, before he could react in anyway, she crushed the snowball in Ethan's face and erupted in laughter.

"Oh, you think you're funny?" Ethan asked in what was meant as a threat.

Wynter squealed and tried to make a run for it as Ethan leaped over his half wall, but she hadn't made it more than three steps when he caught up to her. He wrapped his long arms around her waist. Then with a twist and a turn he tackled her to the ground being careful to keep his own body on bottom.

Wynter screamed and broke out into uncontrolled laughter when Ethan proceeded to tickle her mercilessly.

"Stop! Stop! Stop! Ethan!"

"Wyyynteeer," Noah moaned from beside Ethan's fort wall. "You were supposed to be throwing snowballs at him not letting him tackle you."

"Help me, Noah! Get him!"

That was apparently all the incentive Noah needed, because he started letting Ethan have it with a barrage of snowballs. Ethan, who was still on the ground, loosened his grip on Wynter just enough to defend himself.

Wynter took the opportunity to scoop up a handful of snow and smear it across Ethan's face and down the collar of his coat.

"Hold him down, Wynter!" Noah called.

Wynter quickly turned her body around until she was straddling Ethan's chest. He tried to buck her off, but she held tight.

Noah stood over them with a snowball in hand ready to throw it from that very short distance directly at Ethan's face. "Do you surrender?" Noah asked.

"Never!"

Noah let his snowball fly.

"Ow, hey!"

Ethan bucked again, but this time he flipped his body and Wynter's until she was on bottom and pinned by his large body. "Do you surrender?" Ethan asked. "I've got your precious Wynter."

"You won't hurt her."

"Won't I?"

"No," Noah said uncertainly.

"Don't do it, Noah. Get him," Wynter encouraged.

Ethan wiggled his body about jostling Wynter's, and Noah gasped.

"He can't do anything, Noah," Wynter assured. "He has no hands left, and if he lets go to do anything, I'll get away."

Ethan narrowed his eyes at Wynter challengingly. Then he lowered his face to the crook of her neck and used his head to push back the material of her turtle neck. "I'll bite her. I'll do it, Noah."

Wynter giggled as Ethan's hot breath brushed against her skin tickling as it went.

"Ok, you win. Let her go. We surrender," Noah said on a sigh.

"Ha," Ethan crowed and rolled away to let Wynter up.

Wynter gave Ethan's shoulder a hard shove sending him back down to the snow covered ground. "He wouldn't have bitten me, Noah."

"Couldn't take that chance, though, could you, Noah?" Ethan laughed.

"No, I'm ready to go home." Noah turned away with a sullen and dejected look.

"You cheated!" Wynter spit at Ethan. "That wasn't fair."

"All's fair in love and war." Ethan helped Wynter to her feet. "See you later," he called as he made to follow Noah. What had he meant by love and war?

Noah spent the rest of the weekend pouting. Ethan and Wynter spent the rest of the weekend playing video games.

"He worked really hard on that snowball fight, you know," Wynter said pointedly.

"I noticed."

"He did really good too."

"I know. What did you want me to do? Let him win? He'd still be pouting if he thought I let him win."

"I didn't want you to let him win. I just wanted you to play fair. You cheated."

"He never said biting people was against the rules."

"Ethan!"

"Dad was talking to him last night, and I heard Noah tell Dad that you and I were in league together. He thinks he was double crossed."

"Why would he think that?" Wynter asked indignantly.

"Because you were laughing."

"Laughing? I couldn't help it…Your breath tickled."

"Still."

"Tell him the truth," Wynter demanded.

"I'm not telling him anything. You want him to know the truth so bad, you go talk to him," Ethan shot back.

"Fine, I will."

Wynter found Noah in his room playing with hot wheels. "Can I come in?" she asked.

Noah didn't answer, but Wynter went ahead and sat down next to him anyway. "I know you're upset about what happened, but if it makes you feel any better I think we won. Ethan had to cheat to get you to say we surrendered. He totally would have lost if he hadn't cheated."

Noah still didn't say a word.

"Maybe we can rechallenge him some time."

Noah shrugged. "Don't you want to be on his team next time?"

"No, I liked being on your team. We had fun. Besides, you are much, much better than he is."

"You want to be on my team to be his spy?"

"Noah, what a terrible thing to say! Why would you think that?"

"You helped him win!"

"I most certainly did not! What makes you think I helped him win?"

"Why did you get close enough for him to take you down like that?" Noah challenged.

"He wouldn't come out and fight me face to face. I thought by getting closer I could get the upper hand... You have to remember we're not all as good as you are."

"You really weren't helping him?"

"Nope. I'm kind of mad at him for cheating."

Noah thought about that for a minute. "Ok. There will always be next time when I'm bigger."

"Good."

Wynter stayed for a few minutes more while Noah showed her all his hot wheels. "Wynter? Do you think when I'm grown up, you will marry me?"

Wynter smiled at the unexpected question. "I'll be so old by then you won't want me anymore. You'll want some younger, prettier girl."

Noah shook his head. "You're the prettiest girl I know."

"Thank you, Noah. That's very sweet of you."

"I know I'm still just a kid, but think about it. Ok?"

"Ok," Wynter said softly. "I'll think about it, and you have a good week. Do good on your tests." She kissed the top of his head and stood to leave.

Mrs. Vikki was standing outside Noah's bedroom door. "Thank you," she whispered when Wynter exited.

"No problem."

Chapter Eight

Wynter didn't see much of Ethan or Noah the next week. They both had testing that week at school although for different reasons. So, Wynter spent most of her time with Roscoe who was more than happy to see her home more. It seemed the big lug had missed her.

Wynter and Roscoe were out late one morning playing in a magically enhanced snow flurry when Wynter once again received that eerie watched feeling. This time, however, when she glanced around expecting to see nothing, she saw a tall lean figure in the distance. He appeared to be standing perfectly still and watching Wynter and Roscoe.

As he walked closer, Wynter could see that he wasn't dressed for the weather. He wore jeans, thick obviously lined, and a turtle neck sweater. There was no coat, no hat, no gloves. Wynter and the South Polers stayed warmer than most, but even they needed some extra protection from the elements.

The man was calm. He walked slowly and deliberately. If Wynter had to guess, she would think that the man was taking measured steps to prevent spooking her or Rosco. The man was in clear view now and still moving closer. He was a handsome man. His eyes were such a dark brown that they appeared almost black like his raven locks. He had strong features, and his fitted sweater showed off the contours of hidden muscles.

"Can I help you?" Wynter asked once the man had come to a stop in front of her.

Roscoe had stood his ground; however, he was very tense. Wynter could hear him growling underneath his breath every once in a while. It was clear that Roscoe did not care for this handsome stranger, and he was most definitely handsome. He was the sort of handsome that stole your thoughts away and made you forget to breathe.

"You're not from around here," the man said simply.

"I'm sorry?"

"You're more powerful than a South Poler. So, who are you?"

"Who are you?" Wynter asked indignantly.

"Me? I'm a vampire. My name is Anthony. I detest what I've been forced to do to survive. I've made multiple requests to Santa to undo it, but-"

"Wait, wait, wait. You actually wrote a letter to Santa?"

"Multiple actually."

"You do realize that Santa takes toys to boys and girls, right? Not adults."

"Yes, I'm aware of that, but seeing as how North Polers detest my kind I thought, he might be willing to undo it." Anthony gave Wynter a scathing look then added in a mumble, "Or at least kill me."

"So you're suicidal then?"

"It isn't my first choice, no."

"What are you doing here then?"

"Like I was saying, I have made multiple requests to Santa, but he remains unwilling. As a next resort I fled here. Since magical blood cannot slate the thirst, the South Polers are not threatened by my presence and thus tolerate me. Since there are no non-magical beings here, I'm not a danger."

"Santa can't help you," Wynter felt it her duty to point out.

"He can, yet he won't."

"He doesn't have the power to change what you are. The power that vampires hold to change another is a demonic one. The Clause magic is not demonic."

"You're right in a way. He cannot change what I am; however, he can take away the thirst so that I don't have to have blood to survive."

"You're wrong."

"I'm not. There have been multiple accounts of a Clause giving or taking powers. Thus, I believe he can indeed take away the thirst for blood, but I'll concede that is not what you believe."

"How will you survive here if you have to have blood to survive?" Wynter wondered.

Anthony answered her question with a cold, blank stare.

"You won't. Will you?"

Anthony sighed.

"You came here to die." It wasn't a question, more of an acceptance of fact.

"What else could I do? If I stayed at home, I risked killing again or worse turning some other unwilling victim. Maybe you could help me."

"Whatever it is you believe Santa can do for you, I don't have that kind of power."

"You could talk to your dad for me. Plead my case."

Wynter's eyes widened. "How did you know?"

"I already said that you are more powerful than the South Polers. Since the North Pole magic is only passed through direct blood lines and you are too young to be Santa's wife, you must hence be his daughter. What I don't understand is why you are hiding your magic. It's extraordinary. The way you communicate with the bear, the isolated blizzard you created. You are truly talented, so why hide it?"

"The South Pole residences detest North Polers as much or more than the Clauses hate vampires," Wynter admitted. "They would never let me stay here if they knew."

"Then why stay somewhere you have to hide what you are?" Anthony asked.

"I don't know. Why don't you explain that one?"

"Touché, but I hide because I'm a danger to others. Why do you hide?"

"That's my business."

"Fine, have it your way," Anthony conceded. "So will you do it?"

"Will I do what?"

"Talk to your father."

"No, that's not a good…My father and I…I mean…"

"That's ok. It was a long shot anyway. I don't suppose there's anything you could do is there?"

"No, I'm sorry."

"Don't be. It's not your fault, and the fact that a Clause is even hearing me out is more than I've received up to this point."

Wynter knew that her family had always hated vampires, and unlike with the South Polers, there was good reason. Vampires wielded a demonic power and are driven by a thirst for blood. That alone paints an evil picture, but Anthony…didn't appear evil. In fact, he didn't even act evil. Wasn't he trying to hide from the evil inside?

"I've never met a vampire," Wynter admitted. She wasn't at all convinced that she minded, however. It was nice having someone who appreciated her magic for a change. In the North Pole no one cared. In the South Pole she had to hide. Anthony had already seen several acts of magic, and if anything he acted impressed.

"I pray you never meet another."

Wynter's eyes widened in surprise.

"What you think just because I had evil forced upon me that I don't still believe in and seek God?"

"I...I never thought about it, I guess." A heavy silence fell between them for a moment. "How long have you been here?" Wynter asked trying to fill the silence.

"Not as long as you. It's been nearly a month. You seem taken with the locals already, but you live so far separated."

"You've been watching me," Wynter accused.

"I have." Anthony offered no denial, and he showed no shame.

"Why?"

"You're a transplant who truly does not belong here, yet you have carved out a life for yourself here. I was curious how you did it...I also enjoyed watching you, how easily you wielded your magic and how powerful you are...You won't be able to hide it forever."

"Maybe I won't have to."

"Do you really believe that these people will accept you?"

"They love me."

"Now. That can all change in the blink of an eye."

"What do you know about love? You don't even love yourself!" Wynter gasped and covered her mouth, appalled that she had said such a horrible thing aloud. "I'm sorry. I shouldn't have-"

"No need to apologize."

Roscoe chose that moment to move cautiously closer to Anthony. Anthony watched Roscoe with widened eyes before turning questioning eyes on Wynter. Wynter merely shrugged having no clue what Roscoe was up to. Roscoe sniffed Anthony from toe to head then snuffed loudly in his face before turning and walking back toward the cave.

"What was all that about?" Anthony asked.

"I guess he doesn't see you as a threat."

"You have a polar bear as a guard dog?"

"It beats being alone."

"I'm sure it must," Anthony said on a sigh.

Wynter felt a sympathetic tug at her heart, and even though she didn't want to, she invited Anthony back to her cave. "Would you like to join us for lunch?"

"A Clause and a vampire sitting down to a civil meal together?" Anthony asked with a teasing grin. "I'm afraid I must decline."

Wynter nodded unsure of what else to say and slowly made her way back to her cave. She didn't see Anthony again that week, but apparently others had.

That weekend, Noah met Wynter at the front door. "Guess what! There's a vampire in town."

Ethan rolled his eyes. "I don't know what he's so excited about. It's no big deal. They don't drink magical blood. There's nothing for him to eat around here. He'll either leave or starve. Either way he won't be around for that long."

"Dad said that he can't remember a time in South Pole history when a vampire decided to live here, and Dad would know. He loves history," Noah told. "His name is Anthony Phillips, and he doesn't smile much."

"And, how would you know that?" Wynter inquired.

"I was with Dad when he met the vampire. I think he's lonely. Dad does too. I told Dad that I thought we should be his friends, and Dad said he thought that was a good idea. Mom and Dad said we could go over there today to see him. I asked Mom if she would bake some cookies for us to take, but she said that the vampire couldn't eat them. Will you go with us, Wynter?"

"Oh, I guess I could."

"Come on. Let's get this over with," Ethan said with a put upon expression. "This is all Noah's talked about since they met the guy."

"How old do you think he is?" Noah asked Wynter. "I know vampires don't age. Do you think he's older than Mom and Dad?"

"It's possible."

"That would be way cool! He looks younger than Mom and Dad. I wonder how old he was when he was turned."

It was a short walk from Ethan and Noah's house to the house where Anthony was apparently staying. It was a small place but plenty big enough for one person. It was bigger than Wynter's cave in fact. The house was painted a pale gray color so that it stood out from the white terrain of the South Pole but only slightly.

Noah bounded up the three steps and onto the front porch. He excitedly rang the bell repeatedly until the door swung open. Anthony stood in the doorway wearing nothing but a pair of loose fitting sweat pants. The muscles that his sweater had alluded to earlier in the week were now all on display, and what a glorious display it was. Wynter had never been one to fall for a muscle bound man with no other sustenance, but if anyone could change her mind it was Anthony and his amazing body. Each time she met him, she only saw more to admire. Ironic that demonic power should be housed in such a beautiful temple.

"Hi, do you remember me? I'm Noah and this is my brother, Ethan, and this is our friend, Wynter," Noah said quickly as excitement bubbled from his mouth.

Anthony smiled down at Noah. It was the first smile Wynter had seen from Anthony. That smile should have been award winning. It was the kind of smile that could make a person forget what they were doing. His lips formed the perfect curve showing off teeth that were luminescently white. "I'm pleased to meet you all. What can I do for you?"

Anthony didn't let on that he and Wynter had already met. Relieved, Wynter kept her mouth shut about their previous encounter and prayed that Anthony would keep his mouth shut about her origins.

"We came over to be friendly. My parents say that's what neighbors do. They visit neighbors a lot. Mom wouldn't bake you any cookies, though. She said you can't eat them. Is that true? Can you eat cookies?" Noah wanted to know.

"I'm afraid not. I miss cookies terribly. Won't you come in? It's warm inside."

Anthony turned to lead the way inside and to a cozy living room. Noah was the first to charge in after Anthony. Wynter followed with Ethan bringing up the rear.

"So, this is where you live, huh? Do you live alone?" Noah questioned.

"I do."

"Don't you have any vampire friends?"

"I can't say that I do. We don't always see eye to eye."

"Why is that?"

"Other vampires I've met enjoy being a vampire."

"You don't?" Disbelief rang through Noah's voice.

"No, I don't."

"Why not?"

"Well, despite how movies depict vampires, we are not heroes, and we cannot survive on animal blood."

"You have to have human blood. Do you have people who let you suck their blood?"

"No, drinking from the same person repeatedly is a risk."

"What sort of risk?"

"If I were to drink from them three times they would be turned."

"Oh, cool!"

"Noah," Wynter interrupted.

"Sorry, but it is cool."

"So, it's true that you came here to starve?" Ethan asked.

Anthony gave Noah a nervous glance.

"It's ok. I'm old enough. I can take it," Noah announced.

"Yes, it's true," Anthony answered on a whispered sigh.

Although Wynter already knew the answer, it wasn't any easier to hear the second time. It left a hollow ache in the pit of her stomach. "How long would that take?"

"I'm not sure. I haven't known anyone like me who tried to starve themselves."

"Whoa, what if it doesn't work? What if you won't starve to death at all?" Noah wondered.

"Then I'll cross that bridge when I get to it."

"Yeah, so, how old are you?" Noah asked with no preamble.

A chuckle escaped Anthony's lips before he answered, "Two hundred and thirty-seven."

"Wow, how old were you when you were turned?"

"Barely twenty-five."

"I knew it!" Noah exclaimed.

"You did?" Anthony questioned.

"I knew you looked younger than my parents. You've got a lot of muscles too. Did you already have those muscles when you were turned?"

"My physical state hasn't changed since I was turned, if that's what you're asking."

"So, you were pretty strong before you were turned then."

"I guess I was by human standards."

"Are you stronger now? Do you have like super vampires strength?"

"Yes."

"Could you like pick this whole house up?" Noah dared.

"Only if I wanted to rip it from its foundation."

"I guess that would be a bad idea," Noah conceded.

"A little," Anthony said with a wink.

"So, what else can you do?" Noah demanded.

"I can do most anything you can."

"Can you actually do magic?" Ethan asked.

"A little, but mine is very limited," Anthony admitted.

"What does that mean," Noah asked curiously.

"My magic is mostly to lure someone in to…give blood. It works better on females."

"Can you show us? Wynter doesn't mind. Do you, Wynter?" Noah volunteered.

"Oh, um…" Noah had not grown up with the same distrust of vampires that Wynter had. It was demonic power that Noah was asking Anthony to use on her for crying out loud. Would it tip anyone off if she refused?

"Don't be stupid, Noah. He's saying that his magic is used to seduce women," Ethan chimed in.

"I don't know what that word means," Noah said with eyes narrowed in Ethan's direction.

"It means that my magic would cause Wynter to temporarily fall in love with me," Anthony tried to explain.

Noah eyed him cautiously a minute before asking, "You wouldn't kiss her or anything like that, would you?"

"Of course not."

"And, when you stopped, she would go back to normal?"

"Yes."

Noah turned an eager face to Wynter. "Please, Wynter. I want to see how it works."

"Noah, Wynter might not be comfortable with the situation," Anthony said gently.

"Wynter's not scared of anything. Are you, Wynter?"

Wynter looked at Ethan. Ethan only shrugged one shoulder. "Well, ok," she finally agreed shakily.

"You don't have to do this," Anthony added.

"Please, Wynter, please," Noah quickly pleaded before Wynter could say anything else.

"It's fine," Wynter agreed a second time with more bravado than she really felt.

"Alright…Normally I would spend a few minutes talking to the person so that I am assured she was looking into my eyes. It will save us time if you go ahead and look into my eyes," Anthony instructed.

It was somewhat disturbing that Anthony had an established MO for how he would go about seducing and feeding from some unsuspecting woman. Then again, he had probably done it more than a few times in more than two hundred years.

Wynter obliged by looking Anthony directly in the eyes; although, she didn't expect it to be very effective when they were sitting across the room from one another.

Anthony spoke softly. His voice was soothing and deep. "Wynter, come here please." His words were polite, and he never broke eye contact as he spoke.

Wynter stood and crossed the room to stand directly in front of Anthony. She knew what she was doing. She knew that she was doing exactly what he had told her, and yet she couldn't figure out why she shouldn't.

Anthony patted his lap gently and said, "Have a seat."

He wanted her to sit across his lap. She knew that she was playing right into his hands if she did, but she couldn't resist the chance to get closer to all those delicious muscles. He still had no shirt on, and all those muscles were just begging to be touched. She took another large step forward into Anthony's personal space, but instead of sitting across his lap, she straddled his legs and sat down. Then she scooted up as far as he would allow, trying to get as close as possible to that bare chest of his.

She registered the surprise on Anthony's face, but she couldn't drudge up enough compassion to care. She was just where she wanted to be whether he liked it or not.

Anthony schooled his features quickly and continued. "Wynter, tell me you love me." He sounded like he was begging. How many times had he begged women to tell him they loved him? How desperate he was to find love when he didn't love himself?

Love? Did Wynter love him? Of course not, she had only recently met him. It was far too soon to have fallen for someone so quickly much less a vampire currently wielding his demonic powers. Wynter took a deep breath and let it out on a sigh. "I do. I love you." She leaned forward to kiss him, but Anthony pulled back so that her lips couldn't reach his. He kept eye contact though.

"How much do you love me?" he asked.

"I love you very much." Wynter closed her eyes and leaned in again to kiss him, but somehow she missed.

His lips skimmed across her cheek. Wynter sighed at the sweet caress of his lips. His lips hovered now right next to her ear. "Do you love me enough to share a little of your blood?"

"Yes," Wynter gasped as she grasped Anthony's head and pulled his lips down against the curve of her throat.

Anthony chuckled. "Wynter, look at me." She could feel his lips move against her neck as he spoke. She knew she was going to look at him because he'd asked, but more than anything in that moment she wanted to maintain that contact with his soft, warm, perfect lips.

Wynter drew back and opened her eyes to see Anthony looking back at her, his serious expression interrupted only by a slight grin. He closed his eyes breaking the contact between Wynter and himself, and in doing so he broke the bond.

Wynter could feel the loss immediately. She blinked her eyes a couple times and shook her head trying to make sense of her muddled thoughts. That was when she noticed that she was not only straddling his lap but clinging to him quite inappropriately. She jumped back to her feet and turned away from Anthony to find Ethan on his feet with his fists clinched.

Anthony pushed to his feet, and Wynter turned back to watch him as he addressed Ethan. "I'm sorry if I offended you or caused anything inappropriate. I didn't realize that she would respond quite so vigorously."

"How long does it last?" Ethan growled out.

"How long does what last?" Anthony returned.

Ethan didn't say anything else, but he must have gotten his point across. Anthony glanced down at Wynter and reacted, "Oh! That is a good question. I don't really know. I usually leave women to sleep it off. I simply assumed that when we broke eye contact she would return to normal."

"Come on, Noah. We're leaving," Ethan ordered.

"But, why? That was cool! How did it feel, Wynter?"

"Very..." How did she describe something so sensual to someone so young? "connected," she finished.

Anthony's eyes widened. "You remember?"

"Yes."

"Everything?"

"I think so."

"That's...interesting. No one else has ever remembered."

"Let's go," Ethan demanded again a little louder.

Wynter could hear Noah shuffling toward the front door with a groan as Ethan grabbed hold of her arm and tugged her behind him.

Anthony followed them to the door. "I hope I haven't scared you off. I never meant to be offensive."

"No way!" Noah enthused. "You're cool. Right, Wynter?"

Wynter nodded, but she couldn't figure out why Anthony was looking at her so sadly.

"I'm sorry. I hope you feel better soon," he said.

Wynter felt fine. She laid her right hand upon his chiseled chest, my but that chest was rock hard, and lifted up on tip toe. "Bye," she said just before placing a chaste kiss on his cheek.

Ethan pulled Wynter back as far as his house then instructed, "You go home and sleep, Wynter. I mean it. You don't see him again for at least twenty-four hours. It's probably best if you don't see him alone at all."

Wynter did as Ethan had said. She loved him too much to worry him needlessly. What she really wanted to do, though, was walk right back over to Anthony's and see if he'd let her kiss him now that Ethan and Noah weren't there watching.

It didn't make sense, not really. His spell was over. She knew for fact is was. She could feel the snap as soon as he broke eye contact. Funny, though, how her closing her eyes did nothing to sever the connection.

Still, the spell was over. She should be done with thoughts of kissing Anthony. She wasn't though. As she walked she remembered. His chest was so hard and muscled, and his legs beneath hers had been every bit as firm. His lips were so full. She wanted so badly to feel his lips against hers. He had no doubt kissed countless women over the years; he would be quite the experienced kisser. He must be so good at it. Wynter bet he could teach her a thing or two about kissing.

Wynter sighed. Physical was all the vampire had to offer. Physically she craved him like nothing she had ever craved before, yet she could never love him the way she loved Ethan. She quickened her pace until she arrived back at her cave, and she was asleep within two minutes of her head hitting the pillow.

Chapter Nine

Later that week, Wynter was curled up in the floor with Roscoe reading a mystery novel, when a voice came from outside her cave.

"Hello?" Anthony called.

"What's he doing here?" Wynter asked Roscoe in a whisper.

"For the record, I have very good hearing," he added.

"Come in," Wynter sighed.

"Wow," Anthony murmured as he walked inside. "It looks much smaller from the outside."

"What do you want?"

"I just wanted to make sure you were feeling..."

"Normal?" Wynter provided.

"Yes, exactly."

"I'm fine thank you."

"I can't believe you just curl up with a polar bear like that," Anthony marveled.

Roscoe growled in Anthony's direction. "Hey, I thought we were friends, big guy."

Wynter smiled and nuzzled Roscoe's neck.

"Could I ask you something about the other day?" Anthony inquired.

"Could I stop you?"

"I don't want to make you uncomfortable."

Wynter sighed again. She seemed to do that a lot when Anthony was around. "What do you want to know?"

"You said the other day that you remember what had happened under my spell. Do you still?"

"Yes."

"Were you trying to fight it? Do you think maybe that is why you can remember it all?"

"No, I wasn't trying to fight it at all." That was the truth. She hadn't been trying to fight it. She had just gone with the flow and let it sweep her up.

"Why do you think it is you can remember when others couldn't?"

"I assume you've never tried to work your mojo on another magical being before. I would presume that's all it is."

"That's kind of what I thought too," Anthony said, but his voice had a lilt of disappointment to it. "What was it like? I can't remember when I was on the receiving end of it."

"I could feel the moment we connected. I was completely unaware of everything going on around us after that point. We were the only two that existed for me at that moment."

"Was it like you were being physically forced to do something against your will or more like coercion so that you wanted everything I said?"

"Neither, it wasn't like I had to do something. I felt more-" Wynter cut off immediately when she realized what she had been about to say.

Anthony crouched down in the floor next to Wynter. "You felt more what?" he pushed.

"Nothing. It doesn't matter. I think Noah was really taken with you," she added trying to change the subject.

"It matters to me. I've been trying to figure things out for over two hundred years. You felt more what?"

Anthony wasn't trying to form a magical connection with Wynter. She didn't feel that same bond, but there was something in his eyes that she swore wasn't there before. Somehow she couldn't deny him anything when he had that look in his eyes, or rather she didn't want to deny him anything. "I felt more…uninhibited," she finally admitted as her face turned red. "It felt like there was nothing holding me back from taking whatever I wanted."

Anthony gasped and dropped to his knees.

"There now. Can we talk about something different?" Wynter was trying desperately to look anywhere but at Anthony's face. She didn't want to see the comprehension in his face when he realized exactly what it was she had wanted that day.

Anthony crawled forward, and before Wynter could react his lips were on hers. Merciful heaven! His lips really were warm and soft and everything she had imagined. All too soon his lips were gone when he pulled back and asked, "Wynter? How old are you?"

Wynter swallowed hard and took a deep breath before answering. "Almost twenty-two."

"How old were you when you came here?"

"It-it hasn't been a year."

Anthony sat down next to Wynter with a bone deep sigh that she didn't understand. "What was it like at the North Pole?"

Wynter was taken aback by his strange question and didn't answer at first. Anthony didn't try to rush her. He just waited patiently for her answer.

"The terrain was a lot like it is here."

"I'm not asking about the terrain. What was it like to grow up there?"

After another long pause, Wynter finally answered, "Lonely."

"Didn't you have friends?"

"The elves, the reindeer...The North Pole is home to a very selective few, Santa and his wife and children, the elves, and the reindeer."

"What about school? Didn't you go to school?"

"My mother homeschooled me."

"Do you have any brothers or sisters?"

"Nope, just me."

"But, I thought that the job of Santa was passed down from father to son."

"It is."

"But...?"

"You can imagine my parents' disappointment."

"I'm sure that's not true. I'm sure your parents are very proud of you," Anthony argued.

"My parents probably haven't even begun searching for me."

"So, you ran away from home?"

Wynter turned her head to look at Anthony. "Does that surprise you?"

"Not really. It would have to be something serious to cause a Clause to relocate to the South Pole. I'm assuming you don't want to be found. What I don't understand is why you ran away."

"I couldn't stand it anymore."

"Was it that horrible living in the North Pole?" He made it sound like Wynter had given up Disney Land or something else equally fantastical. "Was it really worth a childish rebellion?"

"This isn't some childish rebellion! This isn't about rebelling against anyone. This is about finding a place in life where I belong."

"So, it had nothing to do with how lonely you felt there with your parents?"

"You have no idea what it's like to be completely ignored."

"No, and you have no idea what it's like to be hated and hunted your entire life."

"No one hunts vampires," Wynter scoffed. "No one even believes in vampires anymore."

"No? What do you think your aunts and uncles are doing right this very minute? Haven't you ever wondered what happens to the Clauses who don't take over the role of Santa, or have you been too busy being the privileged only heir to notice?"

Wynter looked at Anthony with horror. She didn't want to believe what he was saying. She couldn't imagine any of her aunts or uncles hunting someone down and murdering them in cold blood. "Aunt Mary?" the words had squeaked past her lips before she knew what she was asking.

Anthony snorted. "Your Aunt Mary nearly killed me last year."

"She's the baby." And the cute, innocent one. Aunt Mary was short, thin, and adorable. She had blonde hair and the naturally rosy cheeks that most Clauses' do. Her lips were full and pouty, but she wore a smile more often than not. Aunt Mary was always laughing. She was a wonderful playmate when she came for visits. Her visits were rare, but Wynter had always looked forward to her visits. Aunt Mary took such great interest in Wynter's life and spent most of her visits with Wynter. Aunt Mary was mild mannered, patient, thoughtful, respectful, and kind. She never spoke ill of anyone. She never cursed, and she had a soprano voice that dripped with niceness.

"And, a dangerous huntress," Anthony added. Wynter could hear the respect in his voice.

He respected and feared her. A single tear escaped Wynter's eye as she tried to picture her sweet Aunt Mary as a fearsome killer. She turned her face into Roscoe's fur for just a moment wiping the tear away in hopes that Anthony wouldn't see, but she must not have been quick enough or maybe subtle enough. Anthony reached over laying his hand on Wynter's back and gently rubbed in a soothing, circular pattern.

"But, I thought you wanted to die. Why not let one of them catch you?"

"I don't know. Maybe it's the idea of not being able to go out on my own terms. You can't avoid feeling like the monster you are when you're being hunted down like one."

Wynter turned into Anthony's side and wrapped her arms around his waist trying to comfort him the way he had done for her. "Don't worry. You're safe down here. No Clause would be caught dead in the South Pole."

Anthony let his arm return hesitantly to Wynter's back and whispered, "Yeah, that's what I thought too until I ran across you. We're both rebels, I suppose. You're rebelling against your parents, and I'm rebelling against what I am."

"I told you I'm not rebelling."

"Of course you're not," he offered in a patronizing tone as he pulled her tighter against his side.

They sat there wrapped up in each other's arms, in each other's comfort until Roscoe huffed and stood to leave. As Roscoe stood, knocking Wynter off, she fell unceremoniously into Anthony's lap.

"What was that about?" Anthony asked staring after Roscoe.

"Maybe he got hungry and is going to hunt, or maybe he just had to go to the bathroom. He is an animal you know. He's not exactly toilet trained."

"You have a toilet in this cave?" Anthony asked with surprise.

"Yes, I'm not a barbarian," Wynter said scrambling off of Anthony's lap.

"I didn't say you are, but…Wow, how strong is your magic?"

"Strong enough."

"Are you sure you couldn't…you know…help me."

"Yes, I'm sure."

"It's just that your magic is so…incredible."

"I told you it's not possible," Wynter told him again as gently as possible.

Anthony stared Wynter in the eyes for a long moment. "I can't believe that. As long as I believe that it's possible I still have hope."

"Anthony…" Wynter sighed. Who was she to take away his hope? If it made him feel better to believe that her dad could help him but refused, what would it hurt?

"I'm going to go. I'll see you later?"

"Sure. Later. Bye."

Chapter Ten

Saturday when Wynter ran into Noah, he was completely out of breath. "Where have you been? I've been looking for you everywhere," Noah said. "I have to have somebody to go with me if I go over to Anthony's, and Ethan is grounded for two weeks."

"Why is he grounded?"

"For teaching me the word seduce."

"Oh."

"I still don't know what it means, but I went home and told Mom and Dad that Anthony seduced you and they got all kinds of mad. When they found out Ethan taught me that word, they grounded him for two weeks, but anyway, I want to show Anthony my racing game, so I need you to go with me."

"Ok." Wynter may have been in love with Ethan, but it was Noah who she'd follow anywhere. That little boy had completely stolen her heart.

"Hi, Noah," Anthony answered the door a few minutes later. He looked around then added, "I hope Ethan isn't still mad with me."

"Nah, he's grounded for teaching me the word seduce."

"As well he should be," Anthony said with a smile to Wynter.

Noah rolled his eyes and pushed past Anthony into the house. "I brought my racing game for us to play. I'm good though."

Noah spent the morning teaching Anthony how to play the game until he finally announced, "I'm hungry. Do you think we could order a pizza?"

Anthony laughed, "I don't know any local pizza places since I don't eat."

"How about I order and you pay?"

"Sounds fair," Anthony agreed; although, how it sounded fair Wynter didn't ask. It still amazed her that they had pizza places willing to deliver out here in these harsh conditions. They didn't have anything like that in the North Pole. Then again, the North Pole was sort of "top secret."

It didn't take as long to deliver as Wynter would have expected. It was possible that magic played a role in the quick delivery, but Wynter didn't bother to question.

"You have dishes, but you don't eat?" Noah asked as Anthony pulled out plates and glasses for Noah and Wynter.

"It seemed like the normal thing to do."

"Oh. That's very normal of you. Good job," Noah awarded.

When they all sat down at the table together, Wynter dug into the pizza, but Noah sat huddled over his phone.

Suddenly Noah looked up from his phone and asked, "Anthony, do you think you'll ever get married?"

"Oh, um, well, I guess some vampires do get married to one another, but I'm not like most vampires."

"Good. I know what seduce means now, and you should probably know that I'm going to marry Wynter someday."

Wynter froze mid chew at Noah's proclamation.

"So, Wynter is off limits then?" Anthony asked.

"Yep."

"Good to know…Does Ethan know?"

"No, I haven't told anyone yet. I thought I should let you know, though. You know, so that you didn't ruin our friendship or anything."

"I certainly wouldn't want to do that, but aren't you worried about the age difference?"

"What age difference?"

"The one between you and Wynter."

"She's only four years older, ok four and a half years, but there's a bigger age difference between you and Wynter."

"Good point. Just do me a favor, and don't tell your parents you know what seduce means."

"I'm not stupid."

"Good."

Oh boy. It was just an innocent little crush. Those kinds of things happened, right? At least that was what Wynter tried to tell herself all afternoon.

Noah sat right beside Wynter and kept a close eye on Anthony. Noah had no trouble trusting Anthony, the vampire, but Anthony, who could so easily seduce Wynter, was a whole other story.

Noah took hold of Wynter's hand as they walked back to his house that night. "Wynter, what do you think of Anthony?"

"He's alright, I guess."

"Yeah, I like him as a friend, but I mean how do you like him?"

"As a friend," Wynter answered. She appreciated the way Anthony looked and the fact that he was a really good kisser, but Anthony wasn't poor Noah's competition. His very own brother was his competition.

Noah didn't bring it up again, but rather talked about random things as he held tight to Wynter's hand.

When Wynter got back to her cave, Anthony was sitting outside petting Roscoe. "Well, it's nice to see you two have made friends," Wynter chuckled.

"How was your walk home?" Anthony asked pushing to his feet.

"Fine, I think Noah tried to warn me away from you."

At this Anthony laughed as he followed Wynter inside. "He's a cute kid. You have to give him that."

"Yeah, he is."

"You love him don't you?"

"Of course I do. What's not to love?"

"Do you think he knows?" Anthony asked.

"Knows what? That I love him?"

"No, that you're in love with his brother."

Wynter spun on her heel to look at Anthony.

"Your secret's safe with me. It is quite the love triangle the three of you have going on. Noah is in love with you. You're in love with Ethan."

"And you are you in love with?" Wynter asked.

"Me? I'm not in love with anyone but myself. I only forgot how much I crave human affection," Anthony said as he brushed past Wynter. "People who aren't afraid of me. People who don't want me dead. Someone who looks up to me. Someone who doesn't cringe at my touch." On the last sentence, Anthony spun around, twirled Wynter into his arms, and let his lips trail along her jaw line. He twirled her away again as she struggled to draw in each breath. "You know, friends."

"You don't have friends?"

"I do now. I have you and Ethan and Noah."

"You don't have friends your own age."

"Sweetheart, people my age are dead."

"Other vampires?"

"Vicious murderers who enjoy the kill. Why would I want to befriend them?"

"Don't you get lonely?" Wynter pushed.

"Ah, that's the difference in you and me, sweetheart. I've learned that sometimes the loneliness is the better option."

"You think I made the wrong decision running away."

"You ran away from the North Pole from Santa Clause. It's certainly not the decision I would have made, but to each their own."

"You think I should go back."

"That's a decision you have to make for yourself."

"What about Ethan and Noah?"

"What about them. They're going to notice one day. In case you've forgotten, you and I don't age the same as they do."

"You and I don't age the same either," Wynter pointed out. "You don't age at all."

"Too true…Look, I just don't want to see you hurt when the people you love turn on you. It's a little different being ignored by the people you love than it is being hunted by them."

"You don't seriously think that Ethan and Noah would hunt me down, do you?"

"No, but that's not to say that they won't stand by while others hunt you down."

"I wish that I could tell them who I really am," Wynter sighed wistfully.

"The fact that you know you can't, ought to tell you something."

"Would you visit me?"

"Where? At the North Pole?" Anthony reacted.

"Sure, where were you planning to hide me? In the toy factory perhaps?"

Wynter laughed at Anthony's ridiculous sarcasm. "No, that would just be silly. You'd stay in my room where no one would ever look."

Anthony sat down on the bed with a sigh and pulled Wynter down to sit across his lap. "You're a good kid, best Clause of the bunch. I don't want to see you hurt."

"I know...So, do you think Ethan likes me?"

Anthony laughed at the abrupt change of subject. "What am I now, your girlfriend? We sit around and talk about boys?"

"Your honest opinion, what do you think?" Wynter continued to push undeterred.

"My honest opinion?" Anthony sighed.

"Your honest opinion."

"I think he sees you as the sister he never had."

"Yeah," Wynter said sorrowfully, "that's what I think too...when I'm being honest with myself."

"Look on the bright side. You still have the twelve year old, and if that doesn't work out you have me to seduce you," Anthony said with a wag of his eyebrows.

Wynter rolled her eyes. "You're hilarious."

"Tell me more about the North Pole."

"Why are you so interested in the North Pole?"

"I've always been fascinated by the idea of Santa and the North Pole even when I was a kid."

"Especially when you were a kid?"

"Yeah, ok, especially when I was a kid, but I never out grew it."

Wynter stretched out on the bed with Anthony beside her as she told him stories about growing up in the North Pole. She reminisced for hours.

"What about Rudolph? You haven't said a word about him," Anthony pushed eagerly.

"That's because there is no Rudolph."

"Rudolph doesn't exist, but who guides the sleigh?"

"Eight reindeer who were born, bred, and trained to pull the sleigh."

"And, what about those foggy nights?"

Wynter gave Anthony a grin then slowly lifted both her hands from her lap palms up. As she raised her hands, a deep, thick fog rose inside the cave making visibility impossible. With a wave of her hands the fog rolled around creating a tunnel that could easily be seen through. Next, Wynter shone a light that could cut through the fog, and last, she blew out a puff of air from her mouth dissipating the dense fog.

"Why would someone as powerful as Santa need a red nosed reindeer to guide his sleigh?" Wynter asked.

"Good point," Anthony conceded with a melancholy demeanor.

"You're disappointed?"

"I am. I liked the idea of Rudolph finding his purpose and Santa asking for help."

"You know Santa can't do everything on his own," Wynter said bumping her shoulder against Anthony's. "He gets plenty of help from the elves and his wife, even from the reindeer."

"I guess." Anthony pulled Wynter closer, next to his body and rested his lips against her temple. "He just has everything, doesn't he?"

"How so?"

"He has the most wonderful job in the world, delivering toys to excited boys and girls all over the world. He has all those elves and reindeer. He has a wife who loves him and a beautiful daughter, even if you are rebelling right now."

"I'm not rebelling."

"Of course not," Anthony humored her as he pressed his lips to Wynter's temple in a tender kiss. "He has so much love. Even the kids all around the world love him, leaving him cookies and milk. He's surrounded by happiness. Does he even realize how lucky he is?"

"I don't know," Wynter whispered.

When Wynter woke the next morning, Anthony was right there, their faces only inches apart. "Good morning," he greeted.

"Good morning," Wynter returned on a yawn.

"I think we fell asleep."

"Looks like."

"Wynter, could I ask you a favor?"

"What's that?"

"You're Santa's only heir, right?"

"For now."

"Someday when you take your father's place, would you help me?"

"Anthony...I told you. My dad can't help you."

"He can. He knows that too. Someday you'll know it too."

"Anthony," Wynter sighed.

"I know you don't think it's possible, but what would it hurt to try. Can't you promise me that much?"

"The job of Santa has never been passed down to a girl. I don't know that I'll even take over for my dad."

"Ok, so there are a lot of unknown variables. I know it's another long shot, but you're all I have left. If you take over your dad's position one day, will you at least try to help me?"

Wynter nodded, her eyes filling up with tears. "I promise," she whispered.

Anthony pushed up on his elbow then leaned in to kiss Wynter. This kiss was more insistent than their first, and it lasted longer. Wynter closed her eyes and just enjoyed the feel of Anthony's lips moving against her own.

Anthony pulled back and cleared his throat. "I should go. I'm sure you have a lot to do."

In his haste, Anthony nearly tumbled over Roscoe who was asleep in the floor.

Wynter saw Anthony on and off that week while Ethan and Noah were at school, but neither of them mentioned the kiss or Wynter's promise.

Chapter Eleven

Over the next month, Ethan, Noah, and Wynter spent a lot of time at Anthony's house. Winter was setting in, and it was too cold to play outside even for magical beings used to the harsh environment. They played video games, too many video games perhaps. They played hot wheels with Noah, and when the boys were at school, Wynter and Anthony would watch movies.

Although he didn't have a job, Anthony always seemed to have plenty of money which was something Wynter didn't question. He soon took to keeping groceries around the house to appear normal he claimed, but Wynter knew that he did it for her. She had mentioned one day how much she missed fruits and vegetables or even beef, pork, and chicken. Since that day Anthony's fridge and pantry had been stocked. What he kept changed as he learned what things Wynter liked more than others. Having plenty of food at Anthony's, Wynter would spend all day at Anthony's most weekdays.

Sometimes Wynter and Anthony would spend their days at Wynter's cave to be with Roscoe rather than leaving him alone. She didn't want him getting lonely or feeling neglected.

Anthony and Roscoe had become rather good friends by this point. Roscoe almost never growled at Anthony anymore, and he let Anthony get by with more than he let Wynter. Perhaps it was a guy thing. They would play wrestle much more aggressively than Roscoe and Wynter would. Whenever Anthony and Roscoe went to rough housing, Wynter would have to clear the floor for them or risk things being broken.

It was peculiar the way things worked out. She was born a Clause. Now, she was living in the South Pole with her best friend the polar bear, and she couldn't imagine her life without the vampire and the South Pole family who had practically adopted her.

One weekend while Anthony and Ethan played a particularly violent fighting game, Noah grabbed Wynter's hand and held it up in front of his face. After studying her hand for a few minutes he finally asked, "Wynter, how do girls size their hands?"

"What do you mean?" Wynter asked confused by the question.

"How do you know what size ring you wear?"

"Oh, why do you ask?"

"Well…a friend wanted to get you a ring for your birthday and asked me what size he should get, but I didn't know."

"Real smooth," Ethan cackled from where he sat playing the game.

"Shut up!" Noah retorted loudly. "Well, what size do you wear, Wynter?"

Wynter grinned. "You can tell your friend that I where a size six, but he really shouldn't spend too much money."

Noah nodded solemnly more interested in committing the answer to memory than paying attention to how much was being spent. Wynter did hope he didn't spend too much.

Not another word was said about her birthday, which was rapidly approaching. Less than a month away and no one else so much as acknowledged it, but that was fine. They may not have acknowledged her birthday, but everyone was very aware of her presence. She had never felt more loved than she did right there in the South Pole surrounded by friends who by all counts should have been her mortal enemies.

The Saturday morning of her birthday, Wynter set out for Anthony's the way she did most Saturday mornings to meet the guys. No doubt that Ethan and Anthony would be tuned in to some video game already. Those two really were turning into couch potatoes over the winter months.

Wynter opened Anthony's front door and walked on in as normal, but that was the last thing that followed a normal Saturday routine. The foyer was decorated with balloons and streamers. There was no noise coming from deeper inside the house. There were no video games playing; Wynter couldn't hear the TV at all.

She walked further into the house.

"SURPRISE!" Everyone yelled as she walked into the living room, which had also been decorated.

Of course, Anthony was there; it was his house after all. Ethan and Noah were there. Even Mrs. Vikki and Mr. Norm were there, and they were all there to celebrate her birthday. This was by far the greatest birthday Wynter had ever had.

"Were you surprised?" Noah asked.

"I am."

Noah jumped into the air with a whoop.

"Happy birthday, dear," Mrs. Vikki said kissing Wynter's cheek.

Even Mr. Norm gave Wynter a kiss on the top of her forehead and said, "Happy birthday, Wynter."

Ethan hugged Wynter and added, "I can't believe you didn't know something was up."

Noah walked up and pulled Wynter down for a kiss, although not far since he was only a few inches shorter than Wynter now. He kissed her cheek very gently and said, "Happy birthday, Wynter. I love you."

"I love you too, Noah. Thank you. Thank you all so much. I never expected anything like this," Wynter said.

"Happy birthday," Anthony said, and he too kissed her cheek. Wynter could feel Anthony's kiss all the way to her toes. How was it possible that someone whose body temperature was considerably lower than her own could have such warm lips?

Still, it didn't get past Wynter that Ethan had been the only one not to kiss her, and she couldn't help a small frown. Curious, though, was that she caught sight of Mrs. Vikki and Mr. Norm frowning in Anthony's direction.

"Come on," Noah said pulling Wynter further into the room. "Ethan said that you're too old for birthday games. Anthony said you might like dancing, and Mom said that sounded like a lovely idea," Noah mocked. "I think it sounds like a stupid idea, but I'll dance with you if you want to dance."

"I would love to dance with you."

Furniture had all been moved to the side to make room for a dance floor, and Anthony turned on some music. Wynter had a hard time keeping up with Noah's erratic dance moves, but she laughed and had a grand time anyway. Wynter had lost track of how many songs they had danced to when Ethan interrupted.

"Mom needs you in the kitchen," he said.

"Alright," Noah said looking up at Wynter. "I'll be right back. You can dance with Ethan til I get back."

"He's been so excited. I can't believe he hadn't told you already," Ethan said. "The cake was his idea, so act like you love it no matter how frightening it may be."

Wynter danced with Ethan while Noah was in the kitchen with his mom, and Anthony and Mr. Norm sat in a corner talking. He must have been relieved to have another adult to finally talk to. Wynter had never thought about it before. It was strange, though, to think of a two hundred and thirty-seven year old man spending so much time with others so young. Odd that no one had questioned it yet. She would have to remember to ask him sometime why he hangs out with people so young.

Ethan was dancing close, and his full attention was on Wynter. She was so nervous. This was so much more personal than just spending time together.

"Are you having a good birthday?" he asked.

"The best," she smiled back.

"Good…I can't believe Anthony was right about the whole dancing thing. You should make him dance with you. He says he hasn't danced since the late 1800's. Tell him he has to dance at least one song with you since it's your birthday. Noah won't let Anthony squirm out of it if he thinks it what you want."

"Poor Anthony would be putty in Noah's hands," Wynter laughed. It would be funny watching Anthony being controlled by a twelve year old, but Wynter would much rather have danced some more with Ethan.

"I know. It'll be great!" Ethan was eager for his little prank.

"Come to the kitchen, everyone. Cake is ready!" Mrs. Vikki called from the doorway to the kitchen.

The cake was two layers tall and iced in white. It actually looked like a small wedding cake at first glance, but upon further inspection Wynter noticed the… abominable snowmen? They were placed here and there, and there were little balls of icing everywhere that Wynter assumed were supposed to represent snowballs. The balls were scattered around, and some were smashed into the side of the cake.

"What do you think? It's a snowball fight," Noah announced. Noah did love a good snowball fight, Wynter thought to herself.

"Wow, that is so creative," Wynter gushed. Creative and strange, but thoughtful.

The cake and ice cream were delicious, and afterwards Noah insisted that it was time to open gifts.

"Open mine first," Noah said shoving a small box into Wynter's lap.

The small box was wrapped in blue paper. Wynter carefully unwrapped it and discarded the paper. She opened the small hinged box and gasped. A silver ring was nestled inside with a tiny pearl set in the center of the band.

"I thought it looked like a snowball. Do you like it?"

"I love it!" Wynter exclaimed, and she stood to cover Noah's face in dramatic kisses.

Noah pushed Wynter back into her seat and wiped the excess kisses from his face while Mrs. Vikki handed Wynter the next gift.

This one was wrapped in pink paper. This one was bigger but still rather flat. Beneath the paper Wynter uncovered a photo album.

"It's for all your pictures," Ethan explained.

"That's a wonderful idea! Thank you!"

Next came a gift from Mrs. Vikki and Mr. Norm. The box was only slightly larger than the one Noah's ring had come in. Wynter opened the box to find a necklace. Letter charms hung from the chain to spell out her name.

"That's wonderful! Where did you find my name?"

"We had it custom made," Mrs. Vikki admitted with a smile.

"Well, I love it."

The last gift was from Anthony. It was the biggest box thus far, but still lighter than Ethan's had been. Wynter unwrapped and opened a cardboard box to a large stuffed polar bear.

"Maybe you could name him Roscoe," Anthony said with a wink. It was an inside joke since no one else there could possibly know she had befriended a dangerous polar bear.

"You got her a stuffed animal?" Ethan asked with a raised eyebrow in Anthony's direction.

"I didn't know what else to get her," Anthony defended.

"Well, lucky you, now is your chance to make up for it."

"Ethan!" Mrs. Vikki admonished, but Ethan was undeterred.

"Wynter was just telling me earlier that you didn't even ask her to dance. I'll get the music; that is, if you still remember how."

"You do think you're funny, don't you, Ethan?" Anthony replied.

"It's her birthday, Anthony. The least you can do is dance to one little song with her."

Anthony opened his mouth to respond, but before he could utter a sound, Noah was there. "It's her birthday. You have to do what she wants. Just go dance with her. It's not that hard."

Anthony stood with a sigh and reached one hand palm up out to Wynter. She took his hand and let him guide her back to the living room and the middle of the make shift dance floor. The music started to play earning Ethan a scowl from Anthony at his choice of a slow song. Anthony held fast to one of Wynter's hands while he snaked his other arm around her waist. They were dancing much closer now than even she and Ethan had danced.

If looks could kill, no doubt a hole would be searing through Anthony's skull from the look Noah was giving him. Ethan stood by the stereo laughing. Mrs. Vikki and

Mr. Norm had stopped in the doorway to watch. They were now talking in whispers and shooting worried looks Wynter and Anthony's direction.

Anthony was a wonderful dancer as it turned out. He was easy to follow as he glided across the floor. Wynter could barely feel her feet touch the floor. It felt like she was dancing on air as Anthony twirled her through midair holding her securely in his warm embrace. It was actually a lot of fun to dance with Anthony.

After the dance every one helped to clean up. Mrs. Vikki sent Ethan and Noah on home, because they still had chores to do. Then she and Mr. Norm walked home with Wynter.

"Wynter, you know you can tell us anything," Mrs. Vikki said carefully as they started out for their home.

"Yes, ma'am," Wynter answered cautiously. Did Mrs. Vikki know? Had Wynter given away her true origins?

"Has Anthony ever hurt you?" Mrs. Vikki continued.

"No, of course not."

"You know there are more ways for a vampire to hurt someone than just by taking their blood."

"Yes, he's very strong as well," Wynter conceded feeling easier about where this conversation was headed.

"He's very handsome too…Has he ever touched you?" Mrs. Vikki pushed.

Oh! "You mean like sexually? No! Never! Anthony and I are just friends." That excluded the twice now that they had kissed, but there was no way Wynter was going to tell Mrs. Vikki about that.

"Has he ever used his powers on you?"

"Only that once when Noah wanted to see how it worked," Wynter answered truthfully.

"Have you ever been alone with him? Maybe you don't remember him using his powers on you," Mrs. Vikki suggested.

"No, I mean we have been alone before, but I can remember what happened when he used his powers on me. I was aware the whole time of what was happening. There's no way I wouldn't be able to remember him trying it again."

"Are you sure?"

"Yes, ma'am."

"Ok, just remember that we are right here if you need us, dear. If he ever does anything that makes you feel uncomfortable, you tell us right away, no matter how small it may seem."

Well, so much for no one questioning why Anthony was hanging out with people so much younger than him.

Later that night, Anthony came by Wynter's cave.

"Has anyone ever seen you out walking towards my place?" Wynter asked curiously.

"I don't know why?" Anthony replied.

"Mrs. Vikki talked with me on the way home today. She and Mr. Norm are afraid you're taking advantage of me."

Anthony chuckled, which irritated Wynter. What exactly was so funny about that? Was it that absurd to think an older man would want her?"

"If I were them, I'd be more worried about you putting the moves on their teenage son," Anthony said. "Then again they still believe you're seventeen and younger than Ethan."

"Why do you hang out with a bunch of teenagers?" Wynter wanted to know.

"You're not a teenager," Anthony felt compelled to remind her. "You're twenty-two years old. You're a grown adult."

"I'm still considerably younger than you."

"Everyone is. Who would you have me hang out with?"

"I don't know, someone older?"

"Why? Do you feel that I'm a threat to your virtue or maybe Ethan or Noah's?"

"That's not what I'm saying."

"Whatever you're saying, do we have to talk about it tonight?"

"I guess not," Wynter conceded.

Chapter Twelve

"We should have another snowball fight with Anthony," Noah suggested one late afternoon although Wynter wasn't sure exactly who he was talking to. He had been playing with hot wheels while Anthony and Ethan played video games. He seemed to be just musing to himself. "Like we did last time, with forts and all."

"Sure, Anthony can be on my team," Ethan said with a rather wicked grin that was conveniently hidden from Noah.

"Why is Anthony on your team? I wanted to be on a team with Anthony!"

"Three against one? That's not fair. You have to give up one. Either I get Anthony, or I get Wynter."

Noah thought about that for a while before saying anything. He looked over at Wynter rather guiltily then at Anthony. Wynter smiled and said, "Maybe we can switch up and have more than one battle."

"Like we all get a turn to team up with everyone?" Noah inquired.

"Sure, you can team up with Anthony first, and I'll team up with Ethan."

"Is that ok with you, Anthony?" Noah asked.

"That sounds great," Anthony said giving Wynter a knowing grin. For someone so old, he hadn't learned much subtlety over the years.

Everyone started preparing for the first battle as soon as it was warm enough to survive any amount of time outdoors. Just as Wynter knew it would be, Noah and Anthony's fort was going up slowly and elaborately. Their fort looked like an actual fortress complete with little towers. It was very impressive. It was amazing the ingenuity and creativity Noah could come up with, and Anthony's superhuman strength didn't hurt either.

Wynter insisted that Ethan put a little more effort into the fort this time. It would be more fun for Noah that way. Still, Ethan wasn't going to waste time with something as grandiose as Noah's fort. They built snow bricks and built it up into a single wall roughly ten feet long and six feet high.

"You know he's just going to come up from behind," Wynter pointed out.

"Yeah, so?"

"So, aren't you even trying to win?"

"Who said he's going to win that way? I won last time didn't I?" Ethan challenged.

"You had to cheat to win."

"I didn't cheat. There was nothing in the rules that-"

"You knew that was wrong. You used his crush against him."

"Yeah, it was pretty smart."

"Whatever," Wynter said rolling her eyes.

"Are you questioning me?" Ethan demanded with mock seriousness. He gave Wynter a playful shove before fully tackling her into the snow. They rolled around a bit struggling for dominance before Ethan finally got the upper hand.

"Admit my brilliance," Ethan told her.

"You outsmarted a twelve year old. Way to go, big boy."

"Say it. Say, 'Ethan, you're brilliant.'"

"No. Let me up."

"Not until you say it."

"No."

"Ah, do you two need a minute?" a voice interrupted.

Wynter looked up to see a smirking Anthony.

"Wynter was just getting ready to tell me how smart I am," Ethan proclaimed.

"In your dreams," Wynter smiled sweetly.

"There's been a bear sighting in town. The sheriff came by and wants everyone indoors," Anthony told them.

Ethan pushed to his feet and held out a hand to Wynter. "Where's Noah?"

"He's already at the house."

Ethan shot a worried glance at Wynter.

"I'll make sure Wynter makes it home safely," Anthony assured him. "You go on home before your parents get worried."

"Thanks."

Ethan ran off towards his house, and Wynter looked to Anthony. "Is it…"

"No, it doesn't sound like Roscoe. From what the sheriff said, this bear sounds hungry."

Wynter breathed a sigh of relief. "Thank goodness." She hated to think what could happen to Roscoe if he wandered too close to town. A hungry polar bear could do some real damage to the local residents. The rangers would have to put the safety of the people first, but then again the rangers did have a love for the wildlife. Putting the bear down would be a last resort. Just the same, Wynter did not ever want Roscoe to be put in that situation.

"Come on. Let's get you home unless you're looking for a second pet," Anthony coaxed placing a gentle hand on Wynter's back and guiding her along.

"I haven't noticed a food shortage," Wynter said thoughtfully as they walked.

"I could be mistaken. I'm no bear expert. Perhaps he's merely curious, or perhaps he's rather aggressive."

"I guess. Does this sort of thing happen often, you think?"

"I didn't ask. It seemed a little more pressing to get the three of you home safely."

"And yourself," Wynter added. "Aren't you worried for yourself?"

"I wouldn't make a very appetizing meal for a bear. The lack of a warm blood flow, and I've heard that vampire blood is bitter."

"Really? Don't you know for sure?"

Anthony gave Wynter a disgusted look. "I've never drank from another vampire."

"What about your own blood? Haven't you ever sucked blood off your finger after a paper cut or something?"

"No."

"Oh…we'll have to test the theory."

"What?"

"I'm curious now."

"You're curious? Haven't you ever heard that curiosity killed the cat?"

"Yeah, I've heard that before, but true learning starts with a genuine curiosity."

"You're a strange woman, Wynter Clause."

Wynter looked around suspiciously. "Don't say that name aloud out in the open like that. What if someone overheard you?"

"Who's out here to overhear? All sane people are inside hiding from the bear."

Wynter put her arm up to still Anthony. Sitting outside the entrance to her cave was a very large polar bear. It was sitting with its back to them.

"That's not Roscoe, is it?" Anthony whispered.

Wynter shook her head.

"I don't suppose that Roscoe was spending the day indoors?"

Again Wynter shook her head in the negative.

"I want you to get behind me," Anthony ordered and gave Wynter a small, quick shove.

Wynter nearly fell over from the unexpected push, but she wrapped her arms around Anthony and shook her head vehemently. She was not going to get behind Anthony and leave him to take the brunt of the attack. "I'm the one with magic, remember?"

Wynter's whisper must not have been quite enough, because at that very second the polar turned and looked directly at them. Wynter did not know yet what to do. They didn't know that this was the bear from town or even if it was a real threat. Maybe it would leave without harming them. She and Anthony stood perfectly still waiting to see what the bear would do.

The bear stood up and turned in Wynter and Anthony's direction. Anthony snaked his arms very slowly around Wynter in a protective embrace. The bear lumbered toward them. Anthony tightened his grip on Wynter. "Well, do something with all that magic," he pleaded in a breath of a whisper.

"Not yet."

"What do you mean not yet?"

"It's moving too slow."

"What does that mean?"

"It's not in attack mode. I don't want to attack it unless it attacks us."

"By the time it attacks it will be too late."

"Just trust me."

Wynter could feel Anthony's whole body tense up as the bear walked right up to them, and his hold was like a vise.

The bear sniffed Wynter from head to foot then sniffed Anthony foot to head. It snorted blowing snot across both their faces. Then the bear surprised them both by turning and walking away. Neither Wynter nor Anthony moved a muscle until the bear was well out of sight.

"I don't understand," Anthony finally breathed.

Wynter waved her arm in front of their faces ignoring how stiff it was from standing rigid and still for so long. The bear snot disappeared leaving their faces squeaky clean.

"Maybe that was one of Roscoe's friends."

"What does that have to do with anything?" Anthony demanded as he pulled Wynter inside the safety of her cave.

"I think he warned his friends off me once."

"You think?"

"Well, I didn't really understand what was going on, but that had to have been it…That bear must have been one of the bears that sniffed me that day, and you didn't smell like food or a threat."

"One of the bears that sniffed you?" Anthony questioned.

"Yeah."

Wynter was visibly shaken. She was quivering and none too steady on her feet. Anthony sat down on the bed and pulled Wynter across his lap. He rubbed her back in slow, soothing circles. "It's ok. It's all over now. Why don't you tell me about why there were polar bears sniffing you?"

Wynter told Anthony about the day Roscoe had taken her to meet his friends. As she spoke she calmed down.

"Feeling better?" Anthony asked.

"Much."

"Alright, you get some rest, and I'll see you later."

"Thank you, Anthony."

Anthony gave a small nod. "Anytime."

"Be careful," Wynter called after him as he walked out into the cold night air.

They had the snowball fight that weekend mainly because Noah couldn't wait any longer now that he and Anthony had finished their fort. Their fort was a thing of beauty. It was a crying shame that the first blizzard to come through was sure to demolish it the same way the last fort had gone down.

"There have to be rules this time," Noah announced first thing. "No one can hurt Wynter."

"This is a friendly game, isn't it?" Anthony asked. "Surely that rule applies to everyone."

"Well, yeah, I guess, but no threatening Wynter," Noah amended with a scowl aimed at Ethan.

"She's on my team," Ethan pointed out as he wrapped one arm around Wynter's shoulders and pulled her up against him. "Why would I threaten her?"

Noah's eyes narrowed and his brows pulled together for a moment. Then he looked at Anthony and said, "None of that mushy magic stuff."

"I wouldn't dream of it," Anthony replied with a smirk.

"Alright, alright, let's play already," Wynter pushed.

Ethan and Noah counted off ten paces then both teams took refuge at their own fort.

"So what was that about?" Ethan asked.

"Noah?"

"No, Anthony."

"Anthony?"

"Yeah, what was that whole pretty boy smirk about?" Ethan continued.

Wynter really had no idea. Maybe it had been an inside joke between him and Noah. Who knows? "Awe, do you think Anthony's pretty?"

Ethan gave Wynter a shove and said, "You know what I mean."

"Yeah, he is hot. That physique, how could you not notice?"

"Ha, ha, very funny. That's fine. Keep your secrets... Noah's going to blow his top you know."

"About what?"

"When he finds out about you and Anthony."

"What about us?"

"You know he thinks he's head over heels in love with you, and he looks up to Anthony. When he finds out that the two of you are seeing each other..."

"We're not seeing each other," Wynter corrected. How could Ethan have even thought that? As an added kick in the pants, Ethan seemed curious, worried about Noah even, anything but jealous.

"Then what was all that about?" Ethan challenged.

"How should I know? I'm on your team. Remember?"

"Are you playing or not?" Noah yelled interrupting the suddenly uncomfortable conversation.

Wynter turned to attack, but Ethan grabbed her arm stopping her. "Just be careful, ok. Anthony may be interested in more than you are."

"Yeah right."

"Please, Wynter, just be careful. I don't want to have to fight a vampire because he hurt you."

Ethan was openly admitting that he would take on even Anthony for her. That had to be the sweetest thing he had ever said to her. "I'll be careful," she choked out.

Ethan gave one quick nod. "Let's do this on three. One... two... three!"

Ethan and Wynter both ran out from behind the wall. Ethan was immediately beamed with a snowball that Noah had been standing ready to throw. Another snowball whizzed past Wynter's face missing by only a scant centimeter at most, and she could have sworn she saw Anthony wink before he was going for another snowball.

Anthony and Noah were ready for them, and Wynter and Ethan did not hold out long against them. "Maybe me and Anthony are just too good to be teamed up together. You never stood a chance," Noah commented afterwards.

"Sure, kid, whatever you think," Ethan shot back, but Wynter didn't know who Ethan was trying to fool. He hadn't managed to beat Noah yet no matter who they were teamed up with.

"We still have time," Noah pointed out. "You can take Anthony, and I'll take Wynter."

"Fine by me."

So, once again, Ethan and Noah counted off ten paces and each team ran to their fort.

"He didn't hurt you did he?" Noah asked Wynter once they were inside.

"Who?"

"Anthony. I told him I wanted to go after Ethan, but that I didn't want him to hurt you. He's really strong, and he might have thrown one too hard without even knowing it. Are you ok?"

"I'm fine. He didn't even hit me all that much. Most of the time he missed his mark."

"Huh, he threw the game. Oh well, we still won."

"What do you mean he threw the game?"

"I saw him throw before, and he has almost perfect aim."

"Is that so?" Wynter asked as she stormed out of the fortress.

"No, Wynter, come back. We haven't even talked about strategy yet!"

"You threw the game!?" Wynter shrieked as she marched across the distance between the two forts, which was considerably more than last time. You could hardly see one fort from the other.

By the time the wall came clearly into view, both Anthony and Ethan were standing in the open staring at her like she had lost her mind. Wynter didn't know why the thought of Anthony holding back made her so irate, but it did.

"What are you screaming about?" Ethan asked.

"Ask him," Wynter narrowed her eyes at Anthony. Ethan looked at Anthony who shrugged his shoulders looking puzzled. "Noah says you have almost perfect aim," Wynter accused.

"So?"

"So, you missed. A lot."

"I had an off day. What's the big deal?" Anthony asked.

"You missed on purpose. You didn't have an off day. You just didn't think I could handle it."

Anthony picked up a handful of snow and formed a snowball. Next he threw it at a glacier not too far off in the distance. The snowball hit with a thunderous roar just before the glacier crumpled into shards. "No, I didn't think you could handle it," he said with narrowed eyes.

"Whoa, you didn't even put that much behind the swing," Ethan marveled. "Maybe I should put you in charge of knocking down their fort."

"You didn't have to throw it that hard, and you didn't have to miss me on purpose either," Wynter shot.

Anthony took a deep breath. "I think I should call it a day."

"What? No!" Noah cried. "Wynter tell him you're sorry."

"That's fine, Noah. It appears I'm making everyone mad today. I should go."

"Oh come on," Ethan practically growled. "I said I believed you."

Anthony looked at Ethan but didn't say a word.

"You can cover me, and Ethan can cover Wynter," Noah tried desperately.

"I should go," Anthony said and left.

"What did you do this time?" Noah asked turning on Ethan.

"Nothing. I just asked him something."

"What did you ask him?"

"None of your business." Wynter had an idea, though, what Ethan had asked. Since she had not been able to tell Ethan what Anthony's "pretty boy smirk" had been about, Ethan had probably asked Anthony.

Boy, this place was going to give Wynter a complex. The guy she loved only saw her like a sister, and the guy she had kissed got offended if anyone accused him of seeing her. She was starting to feel like a romantic leaper. Anthony probably only felt that way because she was a Clause. What would Ethan say if he knew? He was willing to fight a vampire over her broken heart. That must have counted for something. Surely he could look past who her parents are.

"I'm hungry anyway," Ethan announced and headed toward home.

"I'm sorry I ruined the game, Noah, but that wasn't right. He didn't even give me a chance to prove myself," Wynter apologized, sort of.

"I know. See you later," Noah said before hurrying behind Ethan.

Chapter Thirteen

The next week was one of the loneliest Wynter had known since meeting Anthony. Ethan and Noah were in school, and Anthony was not doing much of anything. She had Roscoe of course, but it wasn't the same as real human interaction.

Even Roscoe was moping about. Wynter had a feeling that he was missing Anthony too. What would her family say if they ever found out she had been pouting over missing a vampire?

That week at school Noah had been introduced to dominoes by a friend, so that weekend he set them up in a trail all around Anthony's house. He had elicited everyone's help.

"Whatever happened to a regular game of dominoes?" Anthony asked idly.

"This is way cooler," Noah told him.

"And way tedious," Ethan added.

"Wait until you see them all fall. It's totally worth it!" Noah thrilled.

Anthony smiled and shook his head.

"What are you so quiet for?" Ethan asked Wynter.

"Am I?"

"You haven't said more than two words at a time since we got here. What's up?"

"Nothing."

"Is everything ok?" Noah asked seriously.

"I'm fine," Wynter assured him. Noah shrugged and went back to setting up his dominoes, but Anthony was not so easily pacified. He arched a questioning brow in Wynter's direction.

Wynter shrugged one shoulder and looked at Ethan who was studying her and Anthony closely. She felt her face blush hot and turned her attention back to the dominoes.

That night they all went over to Ethan and Noah's to eat with their parents. Mrs. Vikki and Mr. Norm cornered her after dinner and asked her again about Anthony.

"Noah said that you and Anthony had a fight last weekend," Mrs. Vikki mentioned casually.

"Yeah, I might have overreacted, but it just made me so made that he was purposely missing me," Wynter admitted.

"Vampires are extremely strong. That sounds very wise and thoughtful of him to go to such lengths to keep you out of harm's way," Mr. Norm noted.

"Ethan said it was nothing. That the two of you would get over it. He seems to think the two of you are getting very close," Mrs. Vikki continued.

"He's a good friend."

Mrs. Vikki nodded. "You haven't forgotten what we said, right? We're here if you ever need us for any reason."

"I know." This was getting out of hand. Mrs. Vikki and Mr. Norm really did think something was going on between her and Anthony. More precisely they thought Anthony was taking advantage of her.

Wynter still didn't fully understand Anthony's motives for hanging out with kids so young…if she could still be considered a kid.

Before they left that night, Wynter looked to be sure no one was paying her any attention. Then she left a magical note in Anthony's pocket asking him to come by her place to talk.

Anthony arrived at the cave only a few short minutes after Wynter. "What's up?" he asked.

"I missed you this week."

"Yeah, I'm sorry about that. I thought if I put a little space between us, Ethan might back off…He threatened to stake me if I broke your heart."

"He didn't!"

"Yeah, I don't think he would really do it. He doesn't have what it takes to be an assassin, but he made his point anyway."

"I'm sorry. I tried to tell him there was nothing going on between us. I don't think his parents believe me either."

"Yeah, I overheard. I thought that might be what this was about."

"You never did answer my question."

"What question is that?" Anthony wondered.

"Why are you hanging out with people so young when you could hang out with anyone in town?"

"Are we back to this again?"

"Yes, you never answered the question."

"Did it ever occur to you that I never answered it because it didn't deserve an answer?"

"It does. I do. I deserve an answer."

"Why do you want to know so badly? I explained last time that there is no one my own age who is worth hanging out with. Are you really that scared of my intentions?"

"Not necessarily; I'm just curious what your motivations are."

"Because, of course, my motivations must be nefarious ones. I would hate for you to live in fear, so let me put your fears at rest." He stormed out of the cave. Wynter knew that if there had been a door, he would have slammed it.

Wynter curled up in bed that night with the bear Anthony had given her for her birthday and cried herself to sleep. She hadn't meant to insult Anthony.

Chapter Fourteen

Weeks went by and there was no word from Anthony. He never came to call at Wynter's cave anymore, and he had refused to answer the door at his house, that had previously never been locked. Not even Ethan and Noah had heard much.

"I miss Anthony," Noah said as he sat in the floor playing with Lego's. Ethan and Wynter were playing video games.

"Me too," Wynter agreed.

"What did you say to him?" Ethan asked. "He said he thought it would be best for everyone if we didn't spend so much time together."

"I didn't…All I did was ask him why he liked spending time with us and not someone older," Wynter admitted.

"Yeah? Well, I think you hurt his feelings," Ethan pointed out the obvious.

"Yeah, you should say sorry," Noah added.

"I would, but he won't talk to me."

"I don't blame him," Ethan said, and if that wasn't what hurt the most.

Wynter waited until late that night when she knew no one would be out and about. She snuck over to Anthony's and knocked on the door. There was no answer. She tried the door, but just like always now, it was locked.

She knocked again, but this time she called out in a whisper, "If you don't answer this door, I'm going to break in. You know I can do it, and there is no one out here to see."

Wynter waited, but Anthony still didn't answer the door. She took one last precautionary look around before waving her hand over the lock and unlocking the door. She walked inside and eased the door closed behind her. "Anthony," she called.

Everything was dark. She had never seen his house so dark. It had an almost menacing quality to it. She wouldn't be scared off though. This was Anthony's house; he would never hurt her. She walked a few more steps before she heard a noise.

"Anthony, is that you?"

Then there was a rumbling. It seemed to be coming from outside. It wasn't Anthony at all. The whole house began to shake.

"Anthony, I'm scared," Wynter called out in a terrified whisper.

"I've got you," Anthony soothed as his arms wrapped around her from behind.

Wynter turned into his embrace and hugged him around his waist. "I'm so sorry," she started, but Anthony cut her off.

"Shh, that's not important right now. Something is going on outside. Let's go." He pulled her outside.

The moon was shadowed by a large sleigh one that Wynter recognized right away.

"No!…That's my father's sleigh."

"Come on," Anthony pulled.

They sleigh hovered over the center of town where everyone was running as fast as their legs could carry them.

"Where is she?" Wynter's mother's voice boomed. "Where is my daughter?"

"We don't have your daughter!" someone yelled back angrily. Wynter couldn't see who it was who yelled, but they sounded more than willing to resort to violence if needed. Everyone standing outside staring up at the North Pole sleigh looked ready for a fight.

Wynter could see the front of the sleigh now. Her mother sat at the helm surrounded by several elves. Her dad was nowhere to be found.

Anthony pushed Wynter further behind himself to hide her.

"What are you doing here, Clause?" someone demanded.

Wynter could see Ethan and his family now not far from where she stood with Anthony. Ethan and his dad were staring at the sleigh with ill intent. Mrs. Vikki was arguing with Noah, trying to get him to go back home and hide.

"I want my daughter," Mom's voice boomed again as if she was speaking into a microphone. "I know she's here, and I'm not leaving here without her. I'll destroy this whole colony looking for her if I have to."

"No!" Wynter gasped.

"Wynter?" Anthony questioned.

"I can't let her hurt anyone...I'm here! Leave them alone!" Wynter called out as loudly as she could, but she couldn't be heard over all the din. When she started to move toward the sleigh, Anthony grabbed at her arm. She looked back at him with a sad expression and whispered, "Take care of Roscoe for me."

"Wynter?" a sad, small voice called.

Wynter looked over her right shoulder to again see Noah. He was staring at her with fear widened eyes. Ethan and his parents were all staring at her as if they could kill her right now if given half the chance. She had never seen such hatred on Ethan's face; she had never considered he was capable of so much hate. The look of hatred was mingled with betrayal and sadness. Anthony had been right all along. They would never accept her knowing who she was.

"I'm sorry," Wynter called out.

Her mother raised her arm as if to start the first attack. Wynter knew it would be brutal, and she feared what could happen to the people whose magic dwarfed in comparison to her mom's. Her mother, however, was a Clause by marriage, not by blood, and her magic could not compare to Wynter's.

A great fire ball flew from Mother's hand and grew in intensity as it raced across the sky toward the buildings below. Wynter raised her own arm and an arch of snow met the fire ball in the sky dousing the flames.

Somewhere in the distance Wynter heard Noah whoop. Everything else went deathly quiet. Wynter transported herself to the sleigh.

"It's about time," Mother said. "I can't believe you made me come all the way down here to get you. Wynter, aren't you ever going to grow up?"

The South Pole people all cheered as the sleigh turned and flew away, but Wynter had grown up quite a bit. She knew now what it was like to have friends. She had loved and been loved in return. Even if they all hated her now, she had been loved for a time. She had learned a great deal about love and friendship. She had also learned a lot about hate and bigotry.

Wynter's mom ranted and lectured the whole way home, but Wynter didn't half listen. She was too busy thinking about how much she would miss all the people she had left behind.

"Why?" Mother asked finally.

"I was lonely," Wynter answered simply.

"Lonely? So you decided to go to the one place where people hate you on sight? How was that any less lonely?"

It was. It wasn't lonely in the South Pole at all. There would be no sense in trying to explain that to her mom, so Wynter didn't try. Wynter, however, knew that had been some of the happiest times of her life.

When they returned to the North Pole, Wynter's dad was still nowhere to be seen. He was probably shut up in his office going over his naughty and nice lists. Wynter knew that was an important task, yet she would have given anything to have been half as important. She ascended the stairs and shut herself in her room. Everything was just as she had left it, yet somehow nothing had stayed the same.

Wynter didn't see much of her parents in her first week back home. Her mother made a point to make sure everyone sat down together for at least one meal a day. She was probably feeling guilty that her only daughter had felt lonely underneath the same roof. The family meals, though, did nothing to dissipate the loneliness.

The whole meal was spent discussing toy production, or reindeer regiments, or even elf satisfaction ratings. Everything still revolved around the job of being Santa. They never just sat down and talked like normal people.

After twenty-two years, Wynter still had no idea what her parents favorite color was. Mrs. Vikki's was red. Mr. Norm liked green. Noah liked blue like his brother, and Anthony preferred black for its simplicity. Wynter had given Anthony much grief over the cliché of a vampire whose favorite color was black.

She had no idea what her parents liked to do for fun. Ethan preferred his video games. If Noah could choose anything in the world it would be to have a snowball fight every day. For all that Anthony protested, he loved to dance. Mrs. Vikki liked cooking, and Mr. Norm had a knack for ice sculpting.

"Dad, have you heard from Aunt Mary lately?" Wynter asked out of the blue one afternoon at lunch.

"Aunt Mary? No, but she is quite adept at taking care of herself."

"I'm sure she is. Why did no one ever tell me before that Aunt Mary is a vampire hunter?"

"I thought you knew," Santa admitted somewhat baffled.

"Well, I didn't. I had no clue, which is not surprising since no one around here talks to me."

"Nonsense, we're talking right now," her dad pointed out.

"What about Anthony? Why haven't you tried to help him?"

"Who is Anthony?" Now her dad looked utterly lost at the turn the conversation had taken.

"He's a vampire."

"Where in heaven's name did you meet a vampire?" Mother asked.

"That's not what's important here. He's a grown man who has written multiple letters to Santa, to you, Dad. He hates what he is, and has asked for your help to undo it."

"I can't change what he is," Santa guffawed.

"That's what I told him," Wynter agreed sadly. "Why do you ignore him, though? Couldn't you show him the least human dignity and tell him so?"

"What is this about?" Santa demanded.

"Nothing, I just thought you should at least tell him you couldn't help instead of leading him to believe you wouldn't help."

"I wouldn't help a vampire even if I could." This was said with a rather haughty attitude that left Wynter wondering if he truly couldn't help Anthony or if he wouldn't. Wynter got the distinct feeling that that was just the case, and it was very disappointing. She was disappointed in her father and heartbroken for Anthony.

Anthony deserved better than what he had been given. He was a good man. He was a kind and loving man. He had looked past age old prejudices that Santa himself was unable or unwilling to move past.

Chapter Fifteen

Wynter couldn't sleep that night. As most nights she got up and wandered down to the kitchen to fix a mug of hot chocolate. While she was warming the water, she heard a sound outside. It was late, too late for anyone to be out and about. Even the toy shop should have been shut down this time of night.

Wondering if one of the reindeer had broken out of the stables, Wynter tied her robe tighter about her waist and pushed out into the harsh night air.

"You shouldn't come out in this weather dressed like that," came a voice from Wynter's left.

Wynter was already leaping toward him before she had even spotted him. "Anthony!" she exclaimed.

Anthony caught her around the waist and hugged her. "This is no easy place to find."

"It's supposed to be impossible if you're not family."

"I guess nothing is impossible when you have faith."

"What about Roscoe?" Wynter worried. "Who is taking care of him?"

"I left him in good hands."

"Whose?"

"Noah, who better to care for a wild beast? Roscoe has already taken to him. Noah gave me a message to give to you. He said he'll always love you no matter what."

That made Wynter smile. "How is everyone else doing?"

"I wouldn't know," Anthony said somberly. "The others are convinced I knew the whole time who you were, and they won't talk to me. They're right of course, but Noah is the only one who doesn't care…That boy sees straight past prejudices. He's going to be a great leader someday…What's this? Don't cry," Anthony said as he wiped tears away from Wynter's cheek.

"Noah really is a great kid, isn't he?"

"Yeah, he is. Let's get you inside before you freeze."

"Ethan hates me," Wynter exasperated as she threw herself down into a chair at the kitchen bar.

Anthony looked around and made himself at home finishing Wynter's hot chocolate and placing it in front of her. "I did try to warn you. Some prejudices just run too deep."

"Why don't you hate me? My family all hunt your kind."

Anthony smiled. "I guess I was desperate enough for help that I kept looking until I saw the real you."

"What are you doing here?" Wynter finally thought to ask.

"A good question," her dad said from the kitchen door where he had apparently been listening for a while.

"Santa," Anthony breathed with all the reverence he could muster.

Wynter rolled her eyes and pushed to her feet.

"Is this the vampire you were talking about?" Santa asked.

"Yes, Daddy, he needs help if you would just try."

"Out of the question," Santa yelled.

"But, Dad-"

"I will hear nothing more on the subject. You have ten minutes to clear out of the North Pole before I call in my sister Mary," Santa told Anthony.

Anthony didn't try to argue. He simply stood there staring at Santa like his childhood hero had let him down, which probably was the case.

"Dad, if you'll only hear him out!"

"Wynter get to your room. Let your father handle this," Mother said from behind Daddy.

"What about Anthony? He's my guest! Daddy, just try!"

"I can't," Santa bellowed. "I'm not strong enough."

"If not you, then who is," Wynter demanded.

Santa gave Wynter a very pointed look. "No!" she cried in denial and made a bee line for the stairs. "No way! I can't do that!"

This broke Anthony out of his stupor, and he turned hurt eyes on Wynter. "You lied. You could have helped me all that time, but you didn't."

Wynter half way up the stairs now, spun on her heels to turn back to Anthony, but the pain she saw on his face stole the very breath from her chest.

"Was I a joke to you? Watch the vampire suffer?"

"No…Daddy tell him…Mother, tell him I'm not strong enough to help him," Wynter pleaded in a whisper, but no one spoke up on her behalf.

Finally her dad spoke up, "Wynter, you're the only one who can help him."

Anger flashed across Anthony's face. "You're no better than him."

Anthony moved to leave, but the indignation of his words had propelled Wynter into motion. She grabbed his face between her hands. "No, you're wrong," she declared before crashing her lips into Anthony's.

She kissed him with everything she had. Everything she had kept pent up. Every longing she had ever felt. She kissed him with all the love she had to give and wished that it were enough to change the way things were.

It didn't take two seconds before Anthony was kissing her back. His hands reached up and clutched her around the waist. Her pulled her closer, and in doing so, lifted her feet right off the stairs. A warm feeling invaded Wynter's body then a blinding light.

Anthony pulled back. "What was that?" he asked.

"I don't know."

"Magic," Santa said like it should have been the most obvious thing in the world.

"Whose?" Anthony asked.

"I don't know," Wynter answered again.

"Come on," Mother said giving Santa's arm a tug. "Let's let them figure this out. I don't think she is in any immediate danger. We'll keep the phone handy in case she is. Mary's only a phone call away."

Wynter got the idea that was as much a warning for Anthony as it was supposed to be soothing to her father. They walked back to their bedroom leaving Anthony and Wynter alone.

"Wynter? Does that mean he's not throwing me out of the North Pole?"

"I have no idea what any of this means," Wynter admitted. "Do you feel ok?"

"Yeah, I feel fine. Are you ok?"

"I'm fine. It didn't do anything to me. I felt warm that was it."

"I felt warm. I felt that kiss too. Are you over Ethan yet?" Anthony asked.

"I'm so over Ethan."

"Think you could get over the whole vampire thing?"

"I'm willing to try if you are," Wynter said then without waiting for his response she wrapped her arms around Anthony's neck and pulled him down for another kiss. One kiss turned into two, and two into four, and four into more until they had both lost count.

Eventually Anthony pulled back with a perturbed look on his face. "Wynter, I'm hungry. I'm so hungry."

Wynter brushed his face with her hand in what she hoped was a soothing gesture. "Anthony, I can't let you kill anyone. You'd never forgive yourself."

"No, I mean I'm really hungry...for food."

"What?"

"I'm hungry. I'm starving."

Wynter smiled. She didn't know what had happened or how, but right now she didn't care. All she cared about was getting Anthony something to eat. "Come on," she said.

Back to the kitchen they went. First she made him a quick sandwich to hold him. Then she started banging around making pasta. Surely pasta would be filling.

"Is everything ok?" Mother asked from the doorway. "Is there anything I can help with?"

"He's hungry, Mother. What does that mean?"

"I think that is something you should ask your dad," Mother said as she moved further into the kitchen to help cook.

Dad appeared in the doorway that Mother had just vacated and cleared his throat.

"Daddy?"

"It means he doesn't need blood anymore. I couldn't help him, because I wasn't strong enough. A Clause will only have magic that strong once in their lives, and I had already used mine when I chose your mother. I changed what she was. She was an ordinary human up until that point...Do you understand what I'm saying?"

"I think so. You're saying that was my magic, and I somehow changed Anthony. So, he's not a vampire any longer?" Wynter questioned.

"No, he's a Clause."

Wynter and Anthony both froze in their tracks surprised by Santa's proclamation.

"He's what?" Wynter finally worked up the nerve to ask.

"He's a Clause," Santa said again with finality ringing in his voice.

"How is that possible?" Anthony asked.

"Every Clause needs a help mate," Santa explained. "So, each Clause has within them the ability to change just one person in their lifetime. You must choose well, because you'll only get one shot at it…I should have explained it sooner, but I didn't see where this was headed."

Wynter tore shocked eyes away from her father and turned to Anthony uncertainly. "Is that ok?"

"I think it's the most wonderful thing I've ever heard," Anthony cheered as he scooped Wynter up into his arms and kissed her soundly. "You know, Noah is going to be very upset with me."

"Who is Noah," Mother interrupted.

"He's a twelve year old with a very big crush on Wynter," Anthony explained. "Any time he felt Wynter and I were getting a little too friendly, he would warn me away telling me he was going to marry her."

"Oh, what interesting people you met while you were away."

Anthony ate enough for two or three people that night. Wynter didn't think he'd ever be satisfied. Wedding plans were started the very next day, but one thing that Anthony and Wynter were very adamant about were living arrangements.

"I think it would be best for everyone involved if we had our own place," Wynter insisted.

"You have plenty of room here," Daddy argued.

"With all due respect, space isn't the issue. Wynter has already run away once. We'd kind of like the chance to start new in our own place," Anthony explained.

"Where would you build?" Mother asked.

"On the other side of the stables," Wynter provided.

"Why so far?" Mother complained.

"We wouldn't want to disturb either of you, and I think there is someone who Wynter would like to bring up from the South Pole first chance she gets," Anthony said with a grin. He knew full well what sort of a reaction he would get to that statement, and the Clause's didn't disappoint.

Their mouths dropped open and Santa said, "Absolutely not. It's out of the question."

"Daddy, Roscoe is a polar bear," Wynter explained before anyone lost their tempers.

"A polar bear? Like a pet?" Santa asked.

"Exactly."

"Well then, of course that is your decision. You said on the other side of the stables, right?"

"Yes," Wynter said as she and Anthony both laughed. Wynter hugged Anthony around the waist, and he wrapped his arms around her. At last, she finally knew her place in life; it was right there with Anthony.

Epilogue

"Wynter, where are you? You know I haven't got long. I've got to check that naughty and nice list one last time," Santa called through the house.

Anthony helped a very pregnant Wynter up off the couch. He and Santa had been working on a Christmas surprise for months, but she had not yet been able to figure out what they were up to. All she knew for sure was that they were excited about it, whatever it was. Wynter waddled her way to the foyer where her dad stood waiting with a tall man with dark hair. His eyes were as blue as a clear winter's sky, and appeared squinted as his huge, infectious smile lit up his face.

It had been just over five years since Wynter had seen him last, but she recognized him immediately. "Noah!" Wynter gathered Noah into her arms over her protruding belly. "What are you doing here!?"

"Surprise!" Anthony whispered softly.

"Good, well, my work here is done, and I have work to do. We're on the eve of Christmas Eve, you know."

"Oh, thank you, Daddy!" Wynter hugged her dad quickly before he left. Then she took Noah by the hand and led him into the living room. "I can't believe it's really you. You look so grown."

"Eighteen now," Noah told her. "Look at you. You're pregnant."

"I am," Wynter said with a loving look at her husband.

"Will you ever forgive me?" Anthony asked Noah. Although Wynter knew that Anthony was partly serious, there was a mocking undercurrent in his tone, because Noah's approval or disapproval wouldn't have changed a thing.

"She looks happy," Noah said with a smile. "I've missed you both."

"How is everyone doing?" Wynter inquired.

"Stubborn as ever," Noah responded. "They're mad that I came, but they could hardly stop me now that I'm eighteen."

"Oh, Noah, I'm so sorry. I never meant to hurt anyone."

"No, I know. The only thing hurting them is their own foolish pride. They refuse to change…even for the better."

"Well, never mind, I'm glad you're here now. How long will you stay?"

"Your dad is going to give me a lift home tomorrow night. He said he would drop me off as close as he could get. Things have really changed since your mom came looking for you. Everyone thought we were vulnerable or some other crap. They've beefed up security. There's only a small group of us that see how silly we've become in this feud."

"Noah, you be careful. It's like someone once told me, some prejudices just run too deep."

"Don't worry, Wynter, I know what I'm doing."

"How did you get here?"

At this Noah looked up to Anthony who smiled around a mouthful of cookie. "No one realizes I'm no longer a vampire, no one but Noah that is," Anthony explained. "It was easy as pie to get in and get him out."

"I bet they're just now realizing I'm gone. When I show back up again for Christmas morning, I'll tell everyone I was out with the wildlife. No one will ever be the wiser. Speaking of wildlife, how is Roscoe?"

"Why don't you see for yourself? He's in the backyard playing in the snow."

Noah walked out with Wynter into the backyard. Roscoe trotted immediately to Wynter's side and began growling lowly at Noah.

"Whoa, calm down, boy. It's me. It's Noah."

Roscoe stopped growling but pushed his way between Noah and Wynter.

"I'm sorry. I should have warned you," Wynter apologized. "Roscoe has been a little over protective since I got pregnant."

"Won't let me near her," Anthony commented as he walked around the three holding a plate of cookies. Roscoe started growling deep in his belly at Anthony, but Anthony only clicked his tongue in a disapproving gesture. "Is that any way to behave toward the one holding all the cookies?"

Roscoe stopped his growling suddenly and plopped to a sitting position with an Earth shaking boom. Anthony popped the rest of the cookie he had been eating into his mouth and held one out for Roscoe. "Here you go."

"You're feeding a polar bear cookies?" asked Noah in astonishment.

"He loves them…almost as much as I do," Anthony defended.

"I don't know how either of them haven't gotten sick off all the cookies they consume," Wynter chided.

Noah burst out laughing. Roscoe and Anthony looked at him curiously, but neither one stopped eating cookies long enough to ask.

"What is so funny?" Wynter finally asked wanting in on the joke.

"Do you remember the first time we all went over to Anthony's together?" Noah asked.

"Yes."

"Remember I had asked Mom to bake some cookies, and she had refused. I asked Anthony if he really couldn't eat them, and he told me that he missed cookies terribly," Noah laughed.

"I did miss them terribly," Anthony said as if there was nothing funny at all, which in turn started Wynter laughing.

"So, what have you been up to, Noah?" Anthony asked.

Noah calmed his laughter down and answered seriously, "A lot, but I'll tell you about that another time. Let's just enjoy the little time we have together," and they did just that.

They stayed up late into the night laughing, talking, and reminiscing. It was the best Christmas present that Wynter had ever received.

Later that night, Wynter hugged her husband close. "I love you, Anthony."

"I love you too, Wynter."

THE *Clause* **REBELLION**

THE *Clause* **REBELLION**

About the Author

Elizabeth Lee Sorrell is an Alabama native. A gifted teacher, she has worked with babies and preschoolers, from her teens all the way to today. She is a teacher in the Federal Head Start program. She has her Associate's Degree in Early Childhood Development, her Bachelor's in Early Childhood Education and Elementary Education, and her Master's in Early Childhood Education.

When not teaching, or leading as the Nursery Coordinator of her church, she is with her family and dear friends, probably reading or writing a book. She loves to spend time with her nieces. Elizabeth is a Christian. She cheers for the Auburn Tigers, and the Atlanta Braves. As a big baseball fan, she has, more than once, written stories in the world of MLB, and watches as many games as she is able.

She enjoys pairing up with Sandra JS Coleman for her covers and illustrations. Sandra, Elizabeth's sister, is a graphic designer and an illustrator.

Learn more at www.ElizabethLeeSorrell.com

Colophon

Cover Design, Cover Photography, and interior
layout designed by Sandra JS Coleman using
Adobe CC software.

The typefaces used on the cover and interior are
Azo Sans Uber, Marydale and Mrs Eaves OT.

Azo Sans Uber was designed by Rui Abreu. He is a
Portuguese type and graphic designer, working on
commercial fonts since 2006. Marydale was designed
by Bryan Willson in 1993. It was his first font designed
based on a friend's handwriting. Mrs Eaves was designed
by Zuzana Licko in 1996. Licko emigrated to the US in
1968 and graduated from Berkeley in 1984.

The book was printed in the United States of America,
on 50lb white paper, perfect bound, with a gloss cover.